TIFFANY T........

The Lost Secret of Dragonfire

The Crystal Keeper Chronicles

Book 3

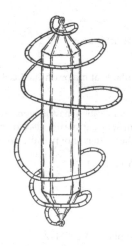

COVER ART AND ILLUSTRATION BY RICH WALLACE

Order this book online at www.trafford.com
or email orders@trafford.com

Most Trafford titles are also available at major online book retailers.

Printed in the United States of America.

ISBN: 978-1-4669-8132-4 (sc)
ISBN: 978-1-4669-8134-8 (hc)
ISBN: 978-1-4669-8133-1 (e)

Library of Congress Control Number: 2013903112

Trafford rev. 02/25/2013

 www.trafford.com

North America & international
toll-free: 1 888 232 4444 (USA & Canada)
phone: 250 383 6864 ♦ fax: 812 355 4082

Dedicated to the connections of friendship
and the memories we share. To Rohan and Grania,
you live on in my memory and my heart.
And to all of my friends and family in my Inner Circle.
Without you, none of this would have been possible.

Contents

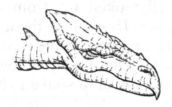

CHAPTER 1

Questions Unanswered

Running. That's what I was doing, with a fire wind on my neck. I didn't know where I was going, but I knew I had to get away. If I looked behind me, I could lose ground. I felt my arms pumping along my sides, as though that would help me go faster. If only I could fly. With that thought, I jumped, leaping over a lump of grass buried along a fence. Faster. Faster. I had to get away.

The air moved through my lungs giving me strength. I wasn't good at running, but the jumping I could do thanks to all my gymnastics classes. I came to what looked like a dead end of the dirt trail I'd been following. I started to examine my surroundings for an exit. A large stone fence seemed to line the edges of my path. At the end was a tunnel. This had to be my escape.

That's when I heard the roar. I didn't want to look back, but sometimes you can't help it. Slowly I turned, feeling like a character in a horror movie as the camera sweeps behind. There it was. A large, scaled creature, teeth bared, with a sinuous neck like a dragon with sweeping Pterodactyl wings. It looked more like a dinosaur from a textbook than a real living thing. It gave another bellow and snorted fire. That can't be good.

My eyes opened. I'd woken up from another of those nightmares. I was glad. This time I thought he might catch me. It's good to wake up just in time, especially when being chased by a dragon. Luckily, it was still only a dream. But it had felt so real. I gave myself a shake to help wake up and focus.

In my line of business, what seems like fantasy can be real. I'm a Crystal Keeper, and between my Fairy Helpers, my talking cat that happens to be a sorcerer too, my unicorn guide, and friends in high places (like the Green Man), dragons could just be around the corner. If these dreams keep coming like this, I won't be surprised if a dragon shows up at the window.

But that's the least of my worries. I still don't know where Edina, my best friend and fellow Crystal Keeper, has been taken. Dark Sorcerer Balkazaar kidnapped her after we fooled him by wishing the Pillywiggin fairies free. I don't think he was too happy about that.

The last time I saw her, Eddie (my nickname for Edina) was grabbed by Balkazaar and taken through a fairy path vortex to who knows where. That's what I've been working on the last few days since I've been back from the fairy paths in Ireland. I've been trying to find her. I have no idea how, but I am going to try.

Since that day, she hasn't been in school. I've called her house, but get no answer. I figured, maybe, in a couple days there would be a big search or something. A newscast would come up with her picture saying she was missing and the girl hunt would be on. But nothing. Absolute nothing. I have no clue what is going on.

Meow.

There was a thump, and I could feel the walking of my cat, Brewford, as he made his way along the bed.

Was it the dream again?

"Yes, Brew, this time he cornered me, and I didn't have an exit. Each time it seems to get worse."

It could be just a symbolic dream. I'm sure you are feeling a bit trapped in your options on where Edina might be. The creature that seeks you could represent your frustrations.

"Maybe, Brew, but somehow I think it's more than that."

Dreams can be messages from other realms. Or sometimes a portent of foreboding. The creature, how would you describe it?

"Scary, big, scaly, and kind of thinking of it, a lot like a dragon."

Dragons are interesting. They can be very helpful sometimes. Did you consider that maybe it's not the dragon going after you, but maybe something else? What do you think you're running from?

"I don't know. I can't see. But maybe I'm not running from the danger, but toward it. Wouldn't be the first time." I gave Brewford a wink.

He gave me a half stare. This seemed to make him look more like Garfield in my mind. With Brewford's striped tail, tabby fur, and Abyssinian eyes, I half expected Odie, Garfield's sidekick, to jump up on the bed next. Of course, Brewford is also a powerful cat sorcerer, not to mention several centuries old, which he never lets me forget. Yoda with fur comes to mind.

Are you ready to feed me? Your mother isn't up yet. I think the second job is making her extra tired.

That's another thing. Mom got a new job that started this week. It's only part time in the evenings, but it's going to make it hard for her to do all the Mom things. You know, helping with homework, cooking dinner, and feeding the cat. So the news went something like this:

"Honey, I'm going to have to rely on you to be more responsible now that I'm working at night too. We need the money, and I know you can do it. 'Kay?"

I simply nodded. I mean what else could I say? I couldn't really tell her the truth. I could see me trying something like this, "Hey Mom, I help the fairies and have saved the world twice now. I can totally handle a night or two a week on my own. I'm a big, sixth grader now, and a Crystal Keeper." But this was a secret I couldn't tell her. No one could know but another Keeper.

But then, being a Crystal Keeper is like that. I have found that saving the day is part of the job. Luckily, I have elves to help with my homework too. One of the perks of being a Crystal Keeper. The elves and other fairies of the realms rely on us to help guard their entrances and assist with magical defense. But that comes later in the story.

Right now, I am just trying to just figure out where Eddie is. It's tough not knowing what happened. I figured, with it being Monday, I could maybe talk to some of her friends I met a few days ago. Maybe they've seen her since last week.

"Okay, hold on, cat." I eased myself off the side of the bed and heard another thump. I felt the rubbing against my legs.

I thought-talk back, *Think that sounded authentic? Gotta keep up appearance, right, Brew.* "After you, Fat Cat," I say out loud. I motion through the doorway as he scuttles through.

Must you use that term with me? I really do think I am quite fit.

"Brewford, you weigh a ton." I keep walking down the hallway until I turn right into the front hall, and then a quick left into the kitchen. "I break my back just trying to pick you up to put you on the couch."

I thought I lost a few pounds trekking though the caves in Ireland.

"No, Brew. You're fat. Just admit it. It's time to get you on a kitty diet. Do they have diet cat food?"

I hear another voice answer my question. It's Mom. "Yes, I think they do. And you're right, dear. I think Brewford has put on a few pounds." Mom turned into the kitchen and went straight to the coffee pot, her morning ritual. "We'll have to look into some weight control dry food at the least."

"Meow!"

Brewford's loud protest made Mom laugh. She looked down and gave Brew a stroke and then returned to pouring water into the coffee maker. "Strange. It's almost like he knows we're talking about him." She gave a big yawn as she pointed to the cupboard. "I put more of his food in the cupboard. I gave him the last can from the fridge last night. You probably need to open a new one." She yawned again. "If you need anything, I'll be in the shower. 'Kay?"

" 'Kay, Mom."

She dashed back through the kitchen doorway, and I was left to feed the hungry cat.

"Meow. Meow." *I have to admit that the tuna is quite nice. Can I have some of that?*

Click. "Oops. I already opened the chicken. Sorry, too late on that order."

Oh well, do remember for next time.

Brew's guzzling sounds told me the conversation was at an end for now. Time for my breakfast. Why does the cat always get fed first? Oh well, better figure out which cereal I want today. Mom had been switching from name brands to the generic cheap cereal sold at the co-op grocery club. It was like Cheerios or Fruit Loops on steroids. Way too much sugar for just one kid. Ah, about just right for me.

The kitchen was filled with happy cat guzzling and cereal chomping sounds. I liked this state of mind—when there is nothing to think about in the morning but eating. I could forget for a while that, so far, I'd failed to find my friend.

Maybe if I headed to the Crystal Store again today, I could find some more clues in the myths and legends section. The Green Man, whom I'd recently visited in the Fairy Realm of Eire, had told me that a lot of truth and wisdom was hidden among the myths and legends of the past. All I had to do was find a clue, something, to find where Eddie might be. It did give me a little hope. I knew I would find her, no matter what.

I finished the last of my cereal as the kitchen filled with the smell of freshly brewed coffee. I could hear the shower still going in the other room. Mom would be a while. I grabbed a clean outfit out of the hall closet and dashed back to my room. For her to make it to work on time, I needed to be ready to leave. Dropping me off at school was one thing that didn't change with her new job.

I was brushing my hair when Brew came in pushing the bedroom door open. *I've been thinking more upon your dream, Wanda. It gives me pause. There is something there. A message, I should think. Only you can decipher it though. Maybe if you try to remember more, you can solve the mystery.*

I kept up with my morning routine. I managed to have my favorite power colors of burgundy and black already picked out in a pair of pants and knit top. My shoes were my plain black, leather tennis shoes. I was thinking it would make me more Goth if I got a steampunk-style pair of shoes. But I still wasn't sure if I could convince Mom yet.

I did a couple more strokes to my boring, brown hair. I looked in the mirror. My glasses were perched on my face. My brown eyes stared back. I couldn't look plainer. You would think that a Crystal Keeper would look more fabulous. Like some hero from some adventure fantasy book. But we look just as plain and normal as everyone else.

"You think there is something to my dreams, Brewford?" I looked down to see him staring in the distance. Cats are notorious for this. But for some reason, I think Brewford is actually looking somewhere else.

He looked back at me, breaking his staring trance. *Most certainly.* He gave his tail a swish to emphasize. *Crystal Keepers must pay attention to their dreams as much as to their studies with magic. Dreams are powerful focusing tools. Your subconscious mind might be picking up on other forces your conscious mind isn't yet aware of. Or it could be a play out of your frustration of not finding Eddie.*

"You really think it is a clue where she could be?"

Possibly. Or a clue for the path you may need to follow. Dreams are a powerful tool for magic. He walked to the other side of the room and jumped on the bed. His eyes were more level with mine as he continued. *What were you planning to do today to find her?*

"I think I'll try asking some of her friends that I met the first day of school. We've been hanging out now and then, especially at lunch. They might have seen her. And maybe visit Mrs. Lawrence at the Crystal Store. Maybe she might have an idea of where Balkazaar would take Eddie, especially since she used to be a Crystal Keeper when she was a kid."

It's a starting point.

We were cut off by Mom's voice coming down the hallway. "Wanda, if you hurry, I can give you a ride to school. It's time, and I'm running a little late. You ready yet?"

"Okay, Mom, I'm almost ready. Be there in a sec," I answered as I was pulling my hair back, into my simple ponytail style. It got my hair out of my face. I wasn't trying to be too fashionable these days, just practical. I didn't have time to be trendy.

I grabbed my backpack and started to go down the hall. Shouting back, I waved to the Brew. "See you after school."

As always. He eased himself into the hallway to watch me go. *Give me a full report when you return.*

"Don't I always," I yelled back as I struggled to strap on the backpack.

"Don't you always what?" said Mom as she opened the front door.

Realizing my mistake, I covered quickly. "Don't I always, ah, do my homework? Should be all ready for another week of school." I flashed a quick smile as my mom shook her head. We headed to the car.

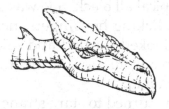

CHAPTER 2

Discovery

Drexel Middle School, home to the slavery of education. Well, at least it feels like slavery when you're eleven and have no choices. The school hadn't changed much since my parents' generation had gone here. The drab, stark building structures in box frames connected by corridors were never that inviting. But school isn't ever inviting. It's just another necessity of life that has to be endured. Sort of like vegetables or doing exercises. There was one smell that gave me hope.

Outside the front of the school were these amazing rosebushes. Their perfume wafted. The scent beckoned me forward. They must be twenty years old. The roses climbed the side wall on a trellis in front of the office. It was something that brightened my morning.

But I didn't have time to enjoy the roses this morning. Mom dropped me in front of the passenger drop-off lane. I got out with my backpack, escaping with a quick wave. I had to find one or two of Eddie's friends before the first bell. I was hoping they might know something.

The sea of students was moving in the direction of the main quad. I blended in with the rest, keeping my eyes peeled for anyone that I might have seen in the last few weeks. Most of Eddie's friends I'd only seen a few times at lunch. They were starting to feel like a regular posse. It's so awesome to finally be part of a group.

I went around the corner and bumped right into Pam. She was wearing her typical all black. She was still chowing down on a breakfast bar, licking her fingers, her nail polish what else . . . black. She looked startled and said a quick, "Sorry." Then she tried to navigate around me. But I turned with a shout, "Hey, Pam, wait up."

"Excuse me." She turned to stare strangely.

"Pam, it's me, Wanda. I'm Eddie's new friend. We met a few weeks ago and were hanging out at lunch. I haven't seen you guys in a few days."

She still looked at me with this weird look. "I don't know you. If you know Eddie, maybe you can't be too bad. But we've haven't met or hung out. You sure you got the right person?"

I was a little stunned. "Well, yeah, we've been eating lunch together a few times a week. Like I think I saw you last Monday. But Eddie and I were busy." I didn't know how to explain saving the world, trying to figure how bees were dying, and fighting an evil dark sorcerer. Fairies rarely work their way into the conversation. "Eddie and I have been out of touch the last few days." I really didn't know how to explain that an evil sorcerer had kidnapped her either. The picture of her being swept away into the light portal will be etched in my mind forever. I shiver. "Studying. We've been doing a lot of research for social studies."

"Well, that's good for you. But I've got to get going." Pam turned to go, her black short hair swung away.

I grabbed onto her sleeve. "Have you seen Eddie in the last week?"

She shook her head. "No, and if I had, I wouldn't tell anyone I didn't know well." She looked at my hand. "So, could you let go. You're kinda weird."

She left quickly after I released my hold on her arm. This wasn't making sense. I knew that we'd been busy researching to solve the mystery of the bees, but we'd been doing lunch with her friends off and on the last few weeks. How come Pam didn't seem to know me now? Something weird is definitely going on.

The first bell rang interrupting my thoughts. I watched Pam, now at the far end of the hall, stop to talk to another girl. The girl turned toward me, and Pam said something to her. They both started to laugh together. The new girl, with her strawberry blonde hair, cut short in a bob looked at me. Her black jeans and burgundy tank top were all too familiar. I'd seen her wear the same outfit when we went researching once at the Crystal Store. It was Eddie.

They sped off laughing and looking back at me. Just then, the second bell rang. I must have stood staring for a while, because a teacher went past me and said, "Shouldn't you be getting to class?" That broke the spell. I hurried to the F-block building. Each building is labeled with a letter. Building F is at the back end of the school.

Luckily, my first class was Literature. I had it with Eddie. Was she going to be there? Or had I just imagined her going off with Pam.

I entered the room looking for her in the corner where we usually sat. There she was. Her familiar strawberry blonde bob leaning over talking to a girl who was the last person I'd have expected. She was talking to Jessica Newark. Jessica. The one girl who had been picking on me for at least a year. Really? Why would Eddie be talking to her? The last time we ran into her, Eddie told off Jessica pretty good for giving me a bad time.

I slowly lowered myself into the seat next to her. Jessica raised an eyebrow. "So, what you looking at, Wanda Weirdo?"

I looked away, and just stared forward. I wasn't going to look back and see if Eddie was looking. I heard whispering beside me. I caught the words "quirky isn't cool" again, followed by "creepy." I tried to sink lower in my seat, willing myself to turn invisible like a fairy. Fairies blend with their surroundings; it was a form of invisibility. I wished I could do it right now. Instead, I sank lower in my seat. I tried to blend with the floor. Then, I heard another laugh.

I turned to the side and shouted, "What?"

More laughter erupted beside me. "Monkey see, monkey do," Eddie said. "See, told you I'd get her to turn around." Then she laughed and turned to Jessica. Jessica had a nasty smile as she joined the laughter.

As far as teachers go, Mr. Trenton is okay. But right then, he seemed like a saint as the door opened and he came gliding to the front swinging his briefcase onto his desk. Chairs moved to face forward; the talking came to a halt. I sat up a little taller. I knew I'd been saved, but more was sure to follow. The school day was starting, and there was nothing they could do while we were in Lit. Class.

Or so I thought. Ten minutes into class, I saw notes being passed around. It started with some giggles behind me. Then, whispers followed with some turn-around stares from kids in front of me. Mr. Trenton sensed something going on and looked up from drinking his coffee. "Is there a problem, Blake, Julie?" They quickly turned back to their journals.

I saw another note get passed from up front to the back row. It traveled a row next to me, and then someone handed it to Eddie. She back grabbed it and lifted it up near her knees. She slowly stuffed it in her black jeans, and then pulled a tissue out of her pocket. She did a dramatic nose blow, held the tissue and note for a sec, and then turned to Jessica to smile. Then, she turned to look at me.

I tried to smile back. When I did, her eyes grew dark. She got this mean and terrible look in her eyes. She wasn't acting like Eddie at all. But there she was in the chair staring at me.

I looked away. This was way too creepy. She thought I was being weird? The last time I saw her, a dark sorcerer was dragging her through a vortex of light. I wasn't sure if I'd ever see her again. And here she was now, sitting next to me as if nothing had happened. Well, maybe something had. Because she wasn't acting like herself.

I turned again to look at her, raising my head slowly. She was looking at me, and not in a good way. She made sure she had my attention before she passed a note to the side. This time, Jessica looked at me, and stifled a laugh. She nodded as if agreeing with Eddie. Then, she noticed Mr. Trenton looking our way, and quickly acted like she was working in her journal.

That's when Mr. Trenton started his policeman walk around the desks enforcing the full twenty minutes of journal time. There weren't any more notes passed for the rest of the period. We spent most of it discussing our current literature assignment; a poem by Edgar Allen Poe called "The Raven." We started to compare him to another poet named Ralph Waldo Emerson. I didn't contribute much, but Eddie took great interest in answering, especially about Poe.

I kept looking at her every time she raised her hand. I mean, Eddie doesn't really like to read. She's more into graphic novels. Yet, she was reciting different lines from last night's reading, like she'd done it. Most of the time, we worked on our homework together, or with the elves. She'd have trouble remembering which poet we were studying. Let alone the actual lines. This just wasn't adding up.

Jessica nodded her head a lot when Eddie said something. As if! Like she actually had the lines memorized or something.

"Tell me, Edina," continued Mr. Trenton, "which was your favorite line in Poe's poem, and why?"

Eddie paused to reflect, like she was really trying to think about it. Then, she turned to Mr. Trenton and smiled, "I don't think I have one favorite line, but I like the fact that the raven keeps answering 'Nevermore,' over and over. As if the guy won't get it. Nevermore, dude, it's nevermore."

Everyone starts laughing, even me a little.

"That's a good way to interpret it, Edina. What do you think is the purpose of the poem, Wanda?"

"Ah," I said, trying to remember it. I'd only glanced over my homework during the weekend. I was really worried about Eddie. One poem, I thought. It can't be too hard. But then, that's when you're always called on.

"Did you read the assignment, Wanda?"

"Kinda. I think I did it Friday, so I don't remember too much except that the raven seems scary, the way it won't let up." There. That was a save.

"Yes, scary seems to be on most of your minds as we start the month of October. That's why I've decided that Poe will be our poet of the month, like Emerson was ours for September. Wanda, I suggest you read the poem again. In fact, let's all take a second look at it together."

As Mr. Trenton walked to the front and everyone opened their books, I heard mumbling to the side of me. Jessica and Eddie had their heads near each other. They had an eruption of laughter behind their hands. I just ignored them. I looked at the clock and noticed we just had a little time until the end of the period. I came up with a plan. While we are changing classes, I can get Eddie alone to talk. I opened my book and tried not to notice the giggles that continued near me.

As the bell rang and Mr. Trenton reminded us to read the next excerpt in our book *The Tell-Tale Heart*, Eddie dashed out with Jessica right next to her, talking up a storm. I couldn't get next to them because of the crush of other students making their way out the door. So I tried another approach.

"Hey, Eddie, wait up."

She called out to Jessica in a loud voice, "Hurry, we don't want the weirdo to catch up with us." They both started walking faster so I ran.

"What is it Eddie? I haven't seen you since . . ."

14

She turned suddenly. "Since I told you that you were a loser, and I didn't want to hang out with you anymore."

"What are you saying? I haven't seen you for the last few days, and I didn't know what had happened."

Jessica interrupted. "The loser doesn't get the clue when people don't want to hang out with her. Get lost, big L."

"Yeah," Eddie added. "Get lost. I don't know what your problem is."

She turned with a huff and walked off with Jessica.

I really didn't know what had happened. Did something happen to her memory? Was she no longer a Crystal Keeper? I watched her go down the corridor. I don't know what is worse, not knowing why she is hanging out with Jessica, or why I have lost my best friend.

CHAPTER 3

Betrayal

I feel like I'm in a void. An ache radiates like I've been hit in the stomach. What happened? We'd worked together to defeat Balkazaar. Why was she acting like this now?

I thought it might be a good idea to ask her at lunch in the cafeteria. The line turns out to be long as I head toward my favorite hot lunch option, pizza. By the time I look for a table, many of the places are taken. I see our group of friends by the back tables near the windows. I head over with my tray.

"Stop right there, freak." I turn to see Jessica come up behind me. "Get out of my way." She shoves by me. I barely have time to scoot backward, balancing my tray to save my chocolate milk.

I watch her head over to the table of my friends. What was going on? Jessica has picked me as her personal enemy. For some reason, I continue to be her target no matter what I say. I've tried to avoid her and not get in her way for two years now. But ever since that gymnastics class we had together last summer, she's been after me. Now she is sitting at the table, and I can't believe it. Her dyed blonde hair flips backward as she settles right next to Eddie.

I start to believe I have entered into another universe. Everything was wrong. I stand there holding my tray, feeling really stupid. If I go over, Jessica will definitely say something. But I have to know. Why is Eddie hanging out with her?

So, I take a deep breath, muster my Crystal Keeper courage, and walk over. I look at Pam and smile. "So, how was everyone's weekend?" There, maybe things can still be smoothed over.

"Get lost wannabe." Eddie's voice feels like a slap in the face.

"I don't know why you think you're our BFF all of a sudden." Jessica's nasal tone carries to the far end of the table. "But get with it. You're totally not with the small hints." The other girls start to look our way. Their conversation stops, and they look at me, then Jessica, waiting.

"I just thought that maybe something had happened that I missed over the weekend. Maybe Eddie knows what happened, you know, in that movie with the unicorn and the evil sorcerer Balkazaar." I tried to talk in code. As a Crystal Keeper, she might remember how she got tricked into the cave, and kidnapped by Balkazaar.

"I don't know what you're talking about." Edina had a strange smile on her face. "So take a hint and leave, w-e-i-r-do." She turns to Jessica and smiles. "I can't believe she thought I was her friend. Shows I must have been out of my mind." They both laugh as I turn to walk away.

I try not to, but I feel the burning of tears. I'm not going to let them see me cry. It isn't fair. She was so cool when I met her a few weeks ago. We'd fought Balkazaar, and then he took off with her. Eddie is my friend. Now she is acting like Jessica's friend. It doesn't make sense. None of this makes sense. Maybe I'm not really a good Keeper after all.

I find a table on the other side by the wall. I shift down near the end where some people have left. There isn't anything to do, but eat. So, I finish just as the bell rings. I dump my things into the trash and leave before I can see Eddie and Jessica leave together.

I endure Math and then Social Studies. All I want to do is sink into the floor. My mind keeps spinning thoughts. Why have I lost my best friend? And to all people, Jessica, the closest thing I had to a nemesis.

Before I know it, the bell rings on last period. I dash out to catch the bus home. It feels empty even though it's full of people. Eddie isn't riding home with me. She usually goes half way before she gets off. Sometimes we go downtown to the Crystal Store to do research. But today, I'm alone. It's the most horrible empty feeling I've felt so far as a Keeper. This hero stuff sucks.

I need to talk to someone. That someone has to be the queen. Yes, I have connections in high places. As Crystal Keeper of the Western Realms, I report to Queen Lillith. She usually has an answer, or could push you onto the path to one.

When I get home, I check my bedroom clock. It reads 4:15 p.m. Luckily, there's enough time for a quick trip to the Fairy World before dinner. "Mom, I'm going out in the orchard to read. I'll be back in an hour."

"Okay, dear, no more than an hour. I'll have dinner ready at five thirty."

I head for the sliding glass door that leads out to our backyard. I scale the fence to land on the dirt clods on the other side. Of course, I've had a lot of practice. I've been climbing over the fence to reach my haven since I was eight. I look down below the trees to make sure none of the farm workers or anyone else is about. Late in the day or out of season, I can expect to have this part of the orchard to myself. Since it is early October, the leaves are changing to the yellow/orange that will later decorate all the trees in the neighborhood. Now, they still cling to most of the branches giving me enough cover to prowl about.

I skirt the rows of trees and make it over to the larger tractor path. It is easier to walk along to get to the "Great Oak."

It isn't really an oak at all, but a really big walnut tree that the neighborhood kids play in. We set up a tire swing a few years ago, and hide it in the top branches when we we're not using it. So far, the farmer hasn't found it. It always seems okay in the spring when we bring it down. But it tends to be filled with leaves and water. The Great Oak is a great place to play. Little did I know it was the secret entrance to the World of Fairy.

I'd found that the fairies love trees as secret entryways. You have to have faith to walk through the trunks, but other than that, they aren't so bad. I step up to the trunk of the Great Oak. I feel along the bark. There are no marks of any kind. It is hard to imagine that I can just step through it when I want to enter the World of Fairy. I hold the crystal pendant. I feel the familiar hum of the fairy crystal's thought voice. *I'm here. The queen will have some direction to follow.* The crystal fairy's voice tingles like bells in my head.

I take a deep breath, and step through the trunk. It takes awhile for my eyes to adjust to the dimly lit passage. It is braced with dark wood surrounded by walls of dirt. Crystals stick out in different directions, and I avoid them easily as I pass. I even know the names of the different types now. That purple one is an amethyst. The yellow one is a citrine. The clear ones are white quartz, and the green-blue crystal is a pale fluorite. Sometimes it is a yellow-green. They are my favorite. A soft glow from the crystals helps light the way.

The path starts to make a hum. A humming grows ahead of me, and I know I am nearing the Crystal Cave. I always like walking the path through here. There are so many crystals at different angles with different colors; it was hard to take it all in. The best thing is the unique choral echo. I whistle.

A breeze of chords erupts. I whistle again, and I'm answered by more notes. I step up my speed through the cave. This isn't a time to enjoy the choral echo. I could lose myself in the sounds if I keep whistling. I'd learned about crystal thrall during some of my studies with the elves. I make it through the maze of passages where the elves live, through the banquet hall, past the meeting hall, and then finally to the Queen's Bowery door.

As usual, it is a solid mass of wood, with no handle. You have to believe to get in. I put my hand on the smooth wood. The grains swim under my fingers as I trace a pattern. Then, I say, "I believe. I wish the door to open to see the Fairy Queen."

The wood evaporates, and there is an opening into another cave filled with amethyst points. Along the floor there is a path of amethyst points leading to a dais near the other end of the cave. On it was a woman that could be anyone's grandmother. She has a kind face, almost like Mother Hubbard. Her monarch butterfly wings extend outward as she steps off of the chair and comes toward me.

"I can feel an imbalance, Wanda. What has happened?" Her wispy purple/blue dress whirls around her as she comes toward me.

"It's Edina, the other Crystal Keeper. She was taken by Balkazaar just a few days ago, and now she's back." I hold back a sniff as my stomach churns. "And she isn't acting like herself at all."

She frowns. "Exactly how is she acting?"

I take a moment. Then, it all comes out too fast. "She used to be my friend and hang out. We were doing everything together. Now she's come back. She's being mean and calls me names. She is totally friends with Jessica. Jessica has hated me since gymnastics class last summer. It's like the last month didn't happened."

"Do you feel better now?" Her grandmotherly voice emphasizes a caring smile.

"Yes. It's been bugging me."

"I can tell, Wanda. For I think your problem has a simple answer. She whom has returned is not Eddie."

"What?"

"I believe Balkazaar has made a switch. He has replaced our Edina with an evil creature called a Doppelganger."

"What is that?" I try not to sound too surprised. But it makes sense now.

"A doppelganger is a creature that is the opposite of someone. If an evil fairy needs someone, they will often replace him or her in the real world with a doppelganger. They look exactly the same as the missing person, but are filled with deceit and bad deeds."

"That would explain a lot." Then I smile. It's simple. "That would mean that Eddie is still my friend. This doppelganger is just making it so no one will notice she's gone."

"Exactly, Wanda." The fairy smiles. "Remember one of the first lessons of being a Crystal Keeper. The best place to start is the beginning. Then, you think it through, slowly and calmly. No need to panic. However, you may need something to verify you've got the answer. I can help you there." She turns and heads out of the Bowery Chamber down a corridor studded with clear crystal points. I follow on her heels knowing if I don't, I'll get left behind. Nothing moves faster than a fairy, especially a fairy with a purpose.

We follow the passage into a torch-lit room. There is no smoke from the fairy light torches. Good thing, because I didn't see where any smoke would go, besides the light is a bluish-green. Guess they aren't your normal kind of torch. The walls are filled with inlaid clear crystals. They glitter and reflect the light like mini mirrors, giving a sparkle rainbow effect to the room. I can see why. The place needs a lot of light, because the room is filled with tables. On the tables are dozens of scrolls laid out in different directions. Along the walls are wooden shelves with different items. Some items sparkle. Others seem to be covered in dust. Whatever the case, the place reeks of importance.

I glance at one of the scrolls. It looks like a scribble. I can't read it.

"What language is this?" I ask.

"Elven," answers the queen. She reaches onto the table and retrieves a pair of glasses from underneath the scrolls. They are wire rimmed with green, round lenses. "These are special, Wanda. They are true-seeing glasses. Try reading a scroll with these."

The queen hands me the green spectacles. Taking off my glasses, I replace them with the green-rimmed eyewear. I look at the scroll she gave me. The swirls are easy to read now.

"I can read a title on the front now. Map of the Elven Lands in the Western Realm." The glasses fall a little forward on my nose. They aren't adjusted to my face. So I pinch the nose guards a bit to get it to fit better. They are amazingly comfortable and light on my face. I look at the queen. She now has a green tinge around her.

The queen smiles amid her green glow. "These glasses see the true meaning of an object. They work wonderfully for reading scrolls unknown to the reader. I think they will work for your purpose."

It takes a moment for me to get it. "You mean, look at Eddie with these glasses?"

"Precisely, Wanda. You will see the truth within her."

"And if it's not her . . ." I smile, the glasses tilt forward a bit. "It will show me something else."

"Most likely what the Doppelganger really looks like." The queen smiles again, with the green glow around her. "For instance, what do you see looking at me?"

"I see you. But with a green glow."

She nods. "Yes. I am in my true state. But if I were to go to the surface and change to my animal form, you would see me instead of a hummingbird." She winks at me.

"These things are great." I look around the room and can read all the scrolls on the walls and book bindings." Titles jump out at me. *Mystical Planes. The Earth and Fairy Kind. What to Do With A Hobgoblin.* Some maps adorn the walls. "Map of the Menehune." It looks a lot like the Hawaiian Islands. I tear myself away. I can spend all day reading these. Shaking my head, I say, "Now what?"

"Give them to me. I'll show you how to put them away safely. They are very delicate." She lifts them off my face, folding the arms carefully together. She picks up a leather case from the table. She places the glasses inside and adds, "Guard them carefully. They can be troublesome in the wrong hands." She hands me the case.

I take them and put the case in my jeans pocket. Then I say, "Thank you, Your Majesty. I think this will help a lot."

The queen snaps her fingers. A fairy with brown hair and eyes appears. I recognize him instantly. I smile and say, "Malik. It's good to see you again."

"Yes, friend Keeper." He bows to the queen. "What does Your Majesty wish?"

"Lead Wanda through our secret passage to the surface. She needs to return quickly so she can get a good night's sleep. She has a doppelganger to expose tomorrow."

He nods and starts to exit the scroll room through another passage.

"What does she mean by quickly? This won't involve bending time again, will it? I can't get grounded, Malik. I need to be home by dinner."

"Do not distress, Keeper. Your time in Fairy has been limited to a few short moments of the above movement circles, or what you call Time. You haven't been missed, yet." He nods with a sneaky smile. Brownies are notorious for keeping you safe in house and home, but as far as being guides, sometimes they get you into trouble. His brown shirt and trousers look like they were a type of home-woven material. Leaves are tucked in and among the weave, and some are even stuck in his hair. He is the embodiment of earthy.

"Lead on, oh great Brownie." I wave forward bowing. "I trust you." I wink at him.

He winks back. "You shouldn't. Remember, I'm notorious. But who else can you trust but your friendly, neighborhood Brownie?" I laugh at this as we continue moving through the corridor. I know he's helped me through a few problems. Not to mention that he's the first fairy I ever met. Malik is a friend.

I start to climb upward, and I have to start bending down. Malik doesn't seem to flinch. "Not to worry, Keeper. Just a bit farther, and we'll be there."

It keeps getting lower and lower until I have to creep along on all fours. The dirt scrapes against my knees as I begin to wonder how much farther. "Hey, Malik, I didn't bring knee pads. How long until we're there?"

A chuckle answers me, as it grows darker. "We're almost to the surface, Keeper. Just a few more crawls, and you'll be home."

We arrive at the entrance, with just barely enough room for me to scoot through. I emerge in my backyard in the corner under our lemon tree. Leaves cover the ground and something skitters away. I still have to bend down since the branches overhead don't give much head room, but at least now I can brush my knees off.

"I can see now why that is a faster way, but less comfortable."

Perfect for Brownies, Wanda.

Brewford's head voice startles me as I clear from underneath the branches of the lemon tree. I step over some border shrubs and am on my patio. Brewford is sitting on the back porch.

"Hi, Brewford. You always ready for trouble?"

Someone has to guard the back porch. Sometimes that entrance isn't just used by Brownies.

I look behind and see Malik's head disappearing under the tree. "Thanks," I yell back. A swirl of leaves is all that's left. I hear, "No Problem," echoing underneath the tree.

"Well, Wanda, I can tell by your face, you found something." Brewford's eyes are in his usual half-open stare. He looks more and more like Garfield every time he does it.

I answer him, "Yes, and I can't wait to try them out."

CHAPTER 4

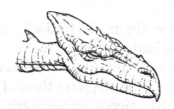

Facing Your Fears

Lunchtime. I have the glasses in my jeans front pocket. I am sitting in the cafeteria waiting patiently for Eddie to enter. The cafeteria hot-lunch line is out the door and slowly moving inward. She should make an appearance any second now. Wait for it.

There. Eddie is standing next to Jessica Newark, there she is, or what must be her doppelganger. We lock eyes and she draws her mouth into an evil smile. Yes. That isn't Eddie. All I have to do is prove it.

I take the glasses out. I look them over for a moment, and then focus my attention back to the lunch line. And she is gone. Jessica is getting her meal in line, but Edina isn't there. I look around the cafeteria. I see Pam dodge into the bathroom. Hmm. I have a hunch.

I get up and head for the girls' room. As I push open the swinging door and see Eddie standing with Pam. Eddie points at me and starts to whisper in Pam's ear. They both are laughing together. I change glasses, putting on the green spectacles as I put my brown-rimmed glasses into the case.

The world becomes green tinted. I look up to see a hideous monster standing next to a green encircled Pam. It has a pale face that is rounded, beady eyes with large, black pupils, and is completely bald. It is wearing Eddie's clothes, but looks like an albino in color. It lets out a shriek when I look at it, and keeps pointing.

"Well, now I know the truth, Eddie." I take the glasses off and see a blur as the Eddie monster rushes me. I didn't expect an attack, and the green truth glasses bounce out of my hands. I hear the crunch as Eddie steps on them. Eddie is smiling at me as she grounds the pieces underneath her foot. Pam lets out a gasp.

"Totally bad fashion choice, Wanda."

I smile back. Everything is still blurry. So I reach for the case and put my glasses on. "You can't be much of a bully now." I smile wider with everything in focus. "Now that I know the truth." I turn and push my way through the door. I almost stumble into Jessica as she shoves past me. I hear her say, "Wannabe."

"Yeah, keep telling yourself that. She's a monster you know."

I smile as Jessica looks at me with a weird look.

I laugh as I walk away, feeling lighter than air. You know, I think I am getting this Crystal Keeper thing.

Later, back at home, I tell Brewford the whole story. I feel so tired from everything. My head is spinning.

Maybe you should lie down. Brewford's thought voice actually sounds concerned. *Maybe a nap would be good.*

"Anything to forget this horrible day. I'd rather get school and the doppelganger out of my head for a while. Eddie is still missing. At least she's still my friend. I know it in my heart."

Brewford gives me a cat rub against my hand. *Rest now. All seems better after a nap.*

"You should know, right? Cats are experts at that."

Napping is very healthy. It keeps balance. So, now, get to it. I'll join you. He curls into a cat ball. I take off my crystal pendant and put it by my nightstand. I always do this when I go to sleep. The crystal hums and warms in my hand. The crystal fairy that lives within is like an advisor from time to time. I've learned that if it gets warm, she usually has a message. I hold it and listen for her head voice. *Sometimes a break from your problems can help you sort them out later. Rest, and all will be well when you awaken.*

Brewford finally gets settled. He has to do three turns to find the right spot. Finally in his cat ball, he starts to purr. The vibration starts to lull me to sleep. I remember thinking before drifting off about Chyra, my unicorn guide in the World of Fairy. She is a master of the fairy paths, and had helped me find Balkazaar's hidden cave. I wonder what she will think about Eddie's doppelganger.

Maybe I just have to rely on my fairy friends now. Malik is a real trickster that loves to give advice when not wanted. Lavendora is another fairy that doesn't seem to trust cats. And then there's Brewford. At least he would be here to help. He's said it often enough.

The last thing I remember before falling asleep was thinking of Chyra, my unicorn guide. She helped me travel on the fairy paths and cross the large waters to Ireland. I remembered riding Chrya on our last adventure. Her fur was soft as a cat. Her sparkles from her golden horn lit the way. I smiled as I drifted off to sleep, relaxing in the memory that unicorns do exist.

Then, I hear laughter. Small giggles at first. It is followed by something being knocked off my nightstand.

HELP! Wanda, help me. My crystal fairy's mind voice screams in my head. I open my eyes to see my little brother standing near my bed. He is holding my crystal pendant and pulling on the cord. He starts swinging it with a big smile.

"Hey, put that down."

With an eruption of laughter, my brother runs out my bedroom and down the hall.

I can hear a scream in my head from my crystal fairy. *Help me. I am flying around and hitting the walls.* My mind fills with a pain like cutting glass.

I grab my temples as I scramble out of bed. I run down the hall and grab him by the shoulders in the living room. "Give it back to me now. MOM!"

"No, it's my pretty necklace now." My brother's toddler voice spits the t's at me. "I found it. All mine."

"No it's not. I put it there when I took a nap. MOM!"

"All right, all right. What has he done now?" My mom circles the distance from the kitchen to the living room. She puts her hands on her hips and looks at my brother. "Jimmy, you're only back for a few hours from visiting your father, and already into trouble I see." He smiles back at her. He tries a "Puss-in-Boots." It's the look like from the movie Shrek, giving my mom the flash of the big brown eyes. My brother gets away with a lot with that look.

"My pretty." He yells out in a long drawn out demand of ownership. "M-I-N-E."

"No dear, it's your sister's necklace. Please give it back."

"No."

"Please, dear, it will make Mommy very happy."

"No."

"Come on you brat, give it back." I am losing my patience.

"Wanda, you have to be gentle with him. He doesn't understand."

"Yes he does. He thinks if he holds anything it's his. That's how he understands."

Mom ignores my quip and continues with her pleading. "Give it to Mommy, and I'll give you a big surprise in return."

His face lights up for a moment. His shaggy brown hair falls in his eyes as his knobby hands flex on the pendant. "What surprise?"

Mom eyes him back leading him into the bait. "A big cookie, just for my little man."

"Cookie." He drops the pendant and toddles into the kitchen. Mom follows as I scoop up my pendant. I look over the crystal pendant. The wire has been broken on one side, and I can see a crack on the bottom point. This doesn't look good.

"Mom, why couldn't he have just stayed at Dad's until Christmas or something?"

I am filled with seething rage. "Why did he have to come back today?"

Mom's voice echoes from the kitchen. "You know the arrangement with your father, Wanda. The month-long visits are supposed to help them bond more as men. Plus, it helps out with the budget and preschool schedule."

"Yeah, this month it's our turn to shuttle him back and forth. I know I'm going to hate October. Can November and December count as one month?" I always get Mom and Dad's crazy mixed-up custody schedule confused. They switch off watching the little terror to help each other's budget. Things were always quieter the month he was visiting Dad. Now the terror of the house was back. I could at least escape during the summer by hopping the fence and reading. But now that he is back, I'll have to make sure everything is far out of reach. I'd lost track of everything just trying to find Eddie and help the fairies.

I look at the pendant again. Yes, there is definitely a large crack at the bottom of the crystal. I hold it to see if I can get any warmth from the crystal fairy within. I thought talk to her, *are you all right? Did he hurt you?*

I feel a massive pain in my head. *I hurt. He has cracked the crystal. You need to take me to the Fairy Queen.* Suddenly, more pain comes rushing between my eyeballs. Ouch. It hurts more than sinus pressure headaches from my allergies.

"Okay, hold on." I whisper as I put the necklace around my neck and look at the clock. Four thirty. There is enough time for a quick trip to the Fairy World before dinner. "Mom, I'm going out in the orchard to read. I'll be back in an hour."

31

"Okay. Be back soon. Dinner will be ready at five thirty."

I head for the sliding glass door that leads out to our backyard. I see my brother round the corner of the kitchen into the living room stuffing his face with a big, chocolate chip cookie.

"Brat," I whisper at him.

"I got a cookie and you don't." He smiles again, but I step out onto the porch and don't look back. That's one thing good about the Fairy World; I can at least get away from my little brother. I hop the fence without looking back.

I rush to the Queen's Bowery. I think the other fairies sense something. Many look in my direction. My crystal fairy's pain rings in my ears. The Bowery Door disappears and I step through.

"I could feel her pain as you entered the Crystal Cave, Wanda. Bring her forth."

I approach the bower chair. The queen steps forward, reaching for the pendant. She turns it about and brings it closer to look at the crack. "She is still alive, but will need to be transferred to a new crystal soon." She cups it in her hands and looks down. She looks it over keenly and sniffs. "Your brother did a fair job of damaging the crystal, Wanda. The crystal fairy will need to be transferred within the next few days, or she will die."

"Die?" I feel stunned as I look at the crystal point in the queen's hand.

"We can sustain her for a while until a new crystal is chosen. But it will need to be soon." Her look is grave, but a curl at her lips conveys her sense of confidence. "You must seek out the Master Miners, the dwarves. They are miners of the special crystals used by our Crystal Keepers. You must go and choose a new crystal for your crystal fairy, before it is too late."

I bite my lip and take a moment. Another fairy problem, except it is my crystal fairy that is at stake, my fairy confidant and friend. She has guided me through so much already. I can't let her down. She is the closest thing I have to a friend besides Edina.

"How do I get a new crystal? I don't know where to start."

"I can tell you where to find the dwarves. They reside in the region you humans call Germany. But you must find your way. Remember, a Crystal Keeper's best allies are friends."

I take a moment. I hate it when the queen talks in riddles. "Well, at least I know Eddie is still my friend. I saw a monster thing when I put on the green glasses."

"And . . ."

"She stomped them. I'm sorry. The monster destroyed the glasses. But I know Eddie wouldn't grab my stuff and destroy it like that. After I knew it wasn't really her, it sort of didn't bother me anymore."

"That's unfortunate. At least now you know the truth . . ."

"I can deal with this new problem. That I have to find the dwarves. And . . ." Then I smile. I'd been thinking of her before I took my nap. Chyra, my unicorn guide, knew the fairy paths like the back of her horn. "Chyra can lead me to the dwarves."

"Good, Wanda. Now you're thinking like a Crystal Keeper." The Fairy Queen smiles at me, placing her hands over the crystal. She closes her eyes, and a light appears between her fingers. "That should keep her stable until you reach the Dwarven Kingdom." She snaps her fingers. Malik appears. This time he seems serious. I didn't think that was possible. "Take Wanda immediately to the surface."

He bows and waves me to follow him. We say nothing as we glide back to the exit under the lemon tree. I think he must have bent time, because before I know it, I am crawling through the secret space under the tree. I emerge to see Brewford on the porch again.

Well, Wanda, I can tell by your face, there is a new problem. Where will this one lead? Brewford's eyes follow me as I get up and brush off some leaves.

I answer him, "Would you believe, Germany?"

CHAPTER 5

A Journey

I continue to fill Brewford in on the situation as we walk through the screen door into the living room. "We've got to get a new crystal for my pendant fairy before she dies. Her old crystal is cracked, and she needs a new one, fast."

And you need my help?

"Well, only if you want to. I know I can't make you do anything."

He sniffs. *No one can make a cat do anything. But so many humans try.* He looks directly at me. *I assume we'll need to call Chyra, your unicorn guide, to help lead us on the fairy paths.*

"Yes, and as soon as possible. The Fairy Queen said time is of the essence." Suddenly, my stomach growls.

He stops to look at me. *By all means, but perhaps after dinner. No one should adventure on an empty stomach.*

I know I'm blushing when I say, "After dinner then. I assume Mom hasn't fed you yet." I follow him as we both move toward the couch.

She seems to have her hands full with your brother. The cat is the last of priorities with toddlers about.

I sit down with a big humph. "And big sisters. Why can't Dad take him longer, I wish."

Brewford jumps up and sits next to me. *There may be a time when you will be thankful that you have a brother, Wanda.*

"I doubt it." I hear scuffling in the kitchen. I give a shout out. "Is dinner ready, Mom?"

"Just a moment, Wanda. In about ten minutes." Her answer is followed by more dishes rattling. "I'll call you when it's ready. Good to see you on time today."

"I'll be in my room." I guess sometimes I do lose track of time, especially when on Keeper business. Besides, I want to see if Brewford knows anything about dwarves. And I want to talk to him without too many ears around. With my brother back, my room might be the only sanctuary left.

I head straight for the covers of my bed. I dive underneath as Brewford hops on at the other end of the bed. He settles into his familiar cat ball position.

"So, what do you know about dwarves, Brewford?" I grab my pillow and lay it on my lap. It's easier to think when I feel comfortable. I look at the Brew, ready for a long lecture.

He swishes his tail once, and begins. *Well, there is a lot of nonsense on dwarves. Mostly legends and myths have contributed to the misinformation.* He raises his head a bit. *But I've never met a dwarf I didn't like. They are gruff and unmannered, but very kind. They are straightforward in their thinking. Plus, they know how to make anything. Dwarves are masters at forging and metal work. Their mines are famous for the most valuable minerals and gems.* He stops and his eyes narrow. *Why are you asking?*

"I have to find them. The queen said they can help me get a new crystal."

Oh dear, that is serious indeed. You'll have need of another crystal before the crystal fairy's energy drains away.

"Drains? The Fairy Queen didn't mention that?"

Fairies don't always give you the whole truth, only the details you may need at the time.

I grab for the pendant still hanging around my neck. I hold it, looking more closely at the crack at the bottom. "She did say I needed to hurry."

Well, there is the truth of it. But the why tends to be left out. Never trust fairies to relay an important message. They'll only deliver what they think is important. He walks over and gives a sniff at the crystal. *It seems the queen has stabilized your fairy friend inside. But we'll need to hurry after dinner. We'll pack to head off to the Dwarven Mines. Chyra will be needed. You can call her then.*

I get my backpack out, and start to put some things in it. I put in a water bottle, change of clothes, and socks. I'm trying to think of anything else I'll need when I hear Mom calling.

"Wanda."

"Think I'll need a compass, Brew?"

We'll have a unicorn, Wanda. Ten times better.

"DINNER, Wanda!" Mom's voice echoes again down the hallway.

I zip the backpack closed. "Okay. Time for food." My stomach rumbles in agreement. I don't have to tell Brewford twice as he follows me down the hall.

After dinner, I call my first emergency meeting. Chyra comes immediately when I send out a mind call for help. Brewford comes bounding back up onto the bed just as a vortex opens in my room. A slow light ball expands into an oval. A white unicorn steps through, her golden horn glints off the light from my wall lamp. She swings her head to look at me with a violet eye. Brewford sits up with his tail swishing to and fro. They look attentive for anything I have to say.

I sit up and lean against my pillow and bed frame. Again, I'm back in the comfortable position that helps me think. I guess that's why I always do my homework spread out on my bed. Desks drive me crazy. So, here I am, sitting on my bed staring at a unicorn and cat trying to figure where to begin. I choose the direct approach.

"I need your help to get me to the dwarves."

I knew it was urgent from your call. Why do you wish to see the Master Miners? Chyra's head voice has the timber of tinkling bells.

I pull the blanket up around me, sitting up. "My little brother cracked my crystal, and I need a new one to save my crystal fairy." I get situated in the right position to listen. I always seem to have trouble sitting or staying in one place.

Of course, Crystal Keeper. I know the path well. My dwarf brothers are well versed in many types of crystals. Which is the one you will need?

"Need? I didn't know I'd need to figure which crystal. I thought they'd just know right off which is the right one."

Brewford's head voice answers my thought. *It's not that you have to find one for your crystal fairy, but that you need to find one for yourself. There are a vast number of crystals from which to choose. She is your crystal fairy. You need to select one for you and her. It should be a crystal that resonates the best with you both.*

Your own magic should resonate with it. Chyra interrupted. *That is the best way to find a crystal.*

"But how will I know?"

You'll know. Brewford gave me a knowing look. *It is something that is hard to explain. It must be experienced. The sooner we go onto the paths, the sooner we will find the right crystal and return.* He nods to Chyra and she comes near the bed.

I stand up and climb onto her back. Holding tightly onto her mane, I wrap my legs around her middle. She has hair as soft as cat fur. Her hooves are golden, matching her horn. Her movement is like a dance. She tips her horn and draws an oval.

An opening of light appears. It grows until it is as tall as my room. I turn and look back. "Brewford, you're coming, right? Of all the times I've needed help, I think this is definitely one of them."

I wasn't hesitating, Wanda. I was reflecting on how easily Balkazaar has kept us from finding Edina.

"Oh, but I forgot to tell you. I used the truth-seeing glasses to see the doppelganger. That thing at school isn't Edina."

Sounds like Balkazaar isn't playing fair again. Chyra's voice rang with concern.

It is something to note. Brewford's whiskers twitch in amusement. *Use of a doppelganger takes a lot of magical energy. It makes me wonder what he is up to.*

"Yeah, Brew, I'm not sure either."

He gave a sniff. *But you'll have to investigate when you return. First you need to save your crystal fairy. One problem at a time to solve is the 3rd rule as a Crystal Keeper.*

"Sometime, Brewford, I'd like to get all those rules written down, but in order from one to where ever they end."

Brewford jumps onto Chyra's back. *It might be hard, Wanda. I don't think there is an end to the list.*

"Why?"

It is a never-ending rule list. Rules get added and taken away as needed.

"Then who writes it?"

You, as you go along.

That's when Chyra steps through the oval doorway of light and we're on the fairy paths.

I don't know how to explain the paths. They are a whole world unto themselves. They are like the crystal cave, but more fluid, and made of energy. Unicorns are masters at being able to navigate them. Chyra is the unicorn that guided me to Ireland when I needed help from the Green Man.

"So which way are we going, Chyra?" I look down the different corridors of light lined with crystals. Rays of energy zip around like errant bolts of lightning. We turn down a path to my left.

We're going to the land of Germany, realm of the dwarves, she answers as she turns down a path lined with smoky quartz points. This path is dark and musty smelling. Dust wafts up from the path as Chyra walks along. The crystals glow a dim grey as we walk along. A small bolt of light whizzes past me. It lights up the path ahead for a second as it goes by us. I can

see its light carrying on down the path as we continue. We follow behind at a slower pace.

"Do we need to go slug speed?" I'm feeling antsy in the saddle.

It is safer to travel the paths slowly, so as to not get lost, answers Chyra as another bolt zips by on the other side.

Yes, Brewford agreed. *We only travel quickly during emergencies.*

"Isn't this an emergency?" My voice squeaks a little, and I feel a little babyish. But I have a feeling we need to go faster. "Can't we speed it up a bit? I want to get the crystal and get back before there are problems with my crystal fairy."

All things in good time, Wanda. Remember, patience sometimes can win over haste. Brewford's head voice rings with somber patience.

I know I can't argue with him. Cats are just too stubborn. "This is starting to sound like another lesson."

I never miss an opportunity to instruct my new Crystal Keeper charge. He sounds smug again, but done with his lecture. He stares forward as I wonder if there was a time he'd ever been humble.

We continue on the smoky quartz path. I can hear Chyra's hooves as we move along. They chime with each step. That's unusual. Most of the time, Chyra is silent. "Chyra, how come your hooves are making noise?"

This path leads down through some of the bowels of the earth, into the Realm of Dwarves. Their capital is in the country you call Germany, but below the surface it is called Felddakar. This path is made more of matter than energy. Since a large part of me is energy, there is a sound while I make contact with more solid earth. The deeper we go, the more I'm grounded. It might even start to make your ears pop soon. Be aware of sudden changes in temperature, too. We may have to go deeper than you are used to.

As we travel down the path, it slowly starts to narrow. I can see the crystals above me starting to get lower and lower. I start to duck down closer to Chyra, her unicorn scent smells of sweet, garden flowers. It's comforting on this deep and dark crystal path. The crystals turn to a darker black as we continue. Chyra's horn glows to light our path.

It begins to grow colder and colder. I start to huddle closer, wrapping my fingers in her mane. My breath starts to fog in front of me.

I feel a shudder go through me as a cool breeze tickles around my feet. We have to be getting closer. I put my arms around myself and start to rub. I didn't put on anything, but a light jacket. I didn't think I'd need more. October is just starting to get cold. Who knew that this journey was going to be so Arctic?

The numbing temperature starts to affect my thinking. I'm feeling a bit foggy. So, I can't resist the question, "Are we there yet?" I really want to get there soon. I'm feeling like a Popsicle.

I do feel the depth of the Fairy World drawing nearer, Crystal Keeper. Chyra's bell like head voice resonates in my head after so much time of silence.

"Good. I was beginning to wonder if I could duck any lower." I eye the smoky quartz crystal jutting above me. I swerve to my left. That was close. "I was thinking we'd have to do the limbo soon."

Limbo, is it a new technique for Keepers? asked Chyra.

Brewford's head voice chuckles. *No, it is a dance to go under things leaning backward. Humans come up with many strange movements to have fun.*

"Well, at least it wasn't the Macarena that I suggested." I'd learned that at my Uncle's wedding a few years ago. I learned the limbo in P.E. Maybe Brewford was right. Humans do weird things for fun.

Brewford starts to turn backward. *Do you feel that, Chyra? There is imbalance along the paths.*

"What?" I chirp up. "What do you mean, Brew?"

There is an imbalance within the fairy paths woven within the earth. I had been sensing it some before, but now it is stronger in the lower paths. His whiskers seem to twitch as he starts to sniff the air.

Chyra's horn grows brighter, trying to light the walls around us. The light seems to be absorbed more than reflected back at us. It's a dull glow that tries to escape each crystal. When the horn grows even brighter, the walls grow even darker. It's all too strange.

"Brewford, there is something weird going on down here." I start to look around some more. I see my dull reflection in the large dark crystal near my head. It grows blurry and disappears. Definitely weird. The cold starts getting even colder. My teeth begin to chatter. I breathe out, and am rewarded with a visible vapor cloud. Clearly, it was getting colder.

We must push forward. Brewford turns around and faces forward again. *I will need to talk to the dwarves about this. They may know what is the cause of the imbalance. I hope it's not too late to correct.* He pats Chyra's back with his paw. *Push onward, Unicorn. Our mission is becoming more than just a crystal search. I fear there may be more afoot.*

We continue through the corridor. Luckily, the path stays at its new height, and I only have to lean forward, with Chryra's mane hair slightly tickling my nose. I start to hear dripping ahead. Slow at first, and than a steady rhythm. We stop suddenly. A glow ahead points like an arrow down the path.

Chyra turns nodding downward. *We've reached the end of this path. You might need help from here on out, since only the dwarves can lead you to the center of their city. Straight ahead you will find it. I will have to leave you here though. This is now dwarf territory. Plus, the path is becoming more material as opposed to being mostly energy. It is difficult for me to go on.*"

"I understand, Chyra. Thank you." I slide off her back, and reach up to hug her. She lowers her head down. It's like hugging a large horse with the softest fur. She is not just any old horse.

She gives a nod. *Good travels to you, Keeper.* Her voice echoes in my mind as she turns and goes back up the path behind us.

Brewford has already gotten down by my feet. He is a fast and sneaky creature. The slight glow of the crystals continues after Chyra has left. It takes a while for my eyes to adjust. I use my hands to guide me. The movement helps generate some heat within me.

I look down at Brew and ask, "So, how do you usually find a dwarf, Brew?"

He walks the path with his tail held high. *Do not fret, Wanda . . .*

A booming voice finishes his sentence, ". . . a dwarf usually finds you."

CHAPTER 6

The Dwarf City

There is a sudden flare of light. Standing in front of us is a shaggy man as tall as me. He has a long, brown beard, a bulbous nose, and beady brown eyes. His eyebrows are beyond bushy, and he holds a torch flooding the corridor with enough light to make the crystals glint in all directions. His clothes look like those of a peasant from a drawing in one of my fairy tale books. You know the look, long flowing sleeves, vest, drawstring at the collar, and brown baggy pants. But the most distinguishing things are his hands. They are large enough that each finger could wrap around my wrist. It makes him look out of proportion. I see the soft, brown leather of boots under the cuff of his trouser.

"Welcome to the City of the Dwarves. For a human child, to be this close, you must be a Crystal Keeper on fairy business. I'm Carlsson of the Watch of the Western Edge of the Dwarf Capital. Be what business ye on?"

I clear my thoughts and stand straighter. He sounded like someone at a Renaissance Fair. Flashbacks of a visit to the

Renaissance Fair come flooding back to me. I try to sound Renaissance Fair-like by saying, "I am a Crystal Keeper of the Western Realms of Fairy. You are right. I have come on some fairy business. I be named Wanda." I point down at Brewford. "This is my cat sorcerer and assistant, Brewford."

Instructor, guide, and general reference for advice. Brewford nods downward.

Carlsson looks me up and down before saying, "What is it that you wish of the Dwarf Kingdom? It is my job to find the best resource to guide ye."

I don't know what more to say. I've only been to a Renaissance Fair twice. Both times, I only talked a bit with some people on the street.

I am struggling to think of something when Brewford says, *Perhaps we can switch to general common speak. I think the old ways have been honored enough.*

I let out a long breath and switch to normal talk. "Well, Carlsson, my little brother totally broke my crystal. I need a new one. My unicorn guide said this was the best place to come."

He answers with a gruff affirmative that ends in a grin. "Good to switch into the informal language. I was never good at the formal language in school, you see. Your unicorn guide was right." He pauses with a new-found confidence in his voice. "We supply the Fairy World with most of their crystals for healing, building, and pretty much anything else they and their Keepers could need them for. If a dwarf knows anything, it's crystals, stones, and the earth. If you need it, we can mine it." He gives me a wink and motions to follow. "I think the Dwarf King would be interested in hearing your problem. Maybe you can help us with ours."

We did notice a magical imbalance in the paths on the way here Dwarf Carlsson. Brewford takes the lead in front of me. He slips right next to the dwarf. *If I'm not mistaken, the energy flow is being interrupted. Have you found the source?*

"That is the problem, Master Cat Sorcerer. We can't find the interruption point. If we knew where it was, we could fix the imbalance. It's as if someone has found a way to divert power from the paths, and it's starting to affect the roots. We need to find it, or the fairy paths themselves will start to collapse. The Fairy World will be divided permanently from the Real World. The imbalance could destroy both worlds."

Brewford makes a tsk tsk sound. *It is more serious than I thought. You're right in taking us to the Dwarf King. I'm going to need to ask some questions.*

This sounds like some kind of Fairy Armageddon. "Do you mean the fairy paths are going to collapse? Be destroyed? How would the fairies travel and communicate?"

It's worse than that, Wanda. Brewford shakes his head as he walks. *The fairy paths connect the World of Fairy, but it is also the conduit for all of the Fairy Magic. Without the fairy paths functioning correctly, Fairy Magic will be cut off or worse, fade from the World of Fairy.*

"And the World of Fairy . . ." I left it hanging in the air as it started to settle into my mind.

. . . would die. Brewford's words were more chilling than the air around me.

Oh boy. Not good. I hope we could find this Dwarf King fast. I don't want to find out what the real world would be like without fairies.

We arrive at the corridor end. It opens up to a glow at the end of the tunnel. I can't speak. We're in a cavern, the largest crystal cave I have ever seen. The walls are lined with crystals, different precious stones and rock. It is beyond a cave dwelling, and anything but cave-man like. It is a catacomb of crystal caves.

In and out of different level openings, dwarves move throughout. Some have beards. Some have long walking sticks, carts, baskets, or even small mules. The rush of industry is about the place, and dwarves are everywhere.

"Welcome to Geldemoor," says Carlsson. He waves his hand about, a smile of pride growing wider. "I can tell this is your first visit to the Dwarf Nation. Your eyes are huge." He puts his thumbs in his belt, and rocks on his boot heels. "Glad that you seem impressed."

"It's an amazing cave!" It is a skyscraper community, complete with ramps connected to a honeycomb of caves. I blink so I'm not too overcome with the sight. "Was it built by dwarves?"

Carlsson starts to take a lower ramp leading through an arch of carved crystal. "Some of these were natural caves that the dwarves mined through. Some of them, we had a little magical help. Over time, the city has grown to the outer districts and mining areas. It will take us a while to get to the center where the king's castle is located."

The ramp leads up and down stairways connecting to more walkways. My head moves upward as I notice arching decorations carved of stone. Colors vary from crystal to black jet. Long drops descend on different sides of the ramp. I look around to see other ramps spiraling near the walls.

I look back to our passage lined by crystals and a dirt wall. On the other side is a ledge. I try to look away, but take a quick peek. I wish I hadn't. It is a direct drop down several levels. I can see the scurrying of dwarves on lower levels moving about their business. I look away, careful to look forward. One wrong step, and splat. It wouldn't be pretty.

I notice warmth easing up from the rocks. I stop having to rub my arms. Heat seems to radiate from the crystals and the wall. I start to stumble, and grab hold of a crystal protruding from the wall. It was one of the biggest crystals. Towering around me are several large clusters that form the arches.

"Those are some of the biggest crystals I've ever seen," I blurt loudly.

"They are made of gypsum. They need water and heat to form. Large parts of the cave were filled with water. As we mined, we drained it away to find some of the largest crystals in our kingdom. They are the largest crystals in Geldemoor."

I nod as I shake my hand. I can feel gentle warmth coming off of the crystals. A dwarf comes from the other direction pushing a cart with large wooden wheels. I make my way close to the wall without bumping the crystals. I nod in greeting and hear a gruff humph. Dwarves are not super friendly.

I keep my eye on Carlsson as traffic starts to increase as we near the center of the city. We come to an intersection with another ramp, and keep heading down. I have to duck around some dwarves to keep up with Carlsson. I can't see Brewford through the scramble of dwarves. I see him emerge in front of me right on track with Carlsson. I know the Brew can move fast when he wants to.

I start to watch the people as they pass by. I notice some dwarves have no beards, and must be female dwarves from their outfits. In fact, the women mostly wear a simple dress that varies in color from rusty orange, browns, and dark crèmes. There is no lace or frilly ornament. But I do notice some jewelry such as a necklace of copper. The men wear mostly belts and the occasional copper ring. And I don't see many children. A few would scamper behind their mothers, or peek behind a dress. But they seem awfully shy. Strange. Maybe it's just me.

"Where are all the kids, Carlsson? Are they in school or something?"

"Why yes, Wanda. Time in the caves is different than in the human world. Our children grow up quickly, three to five years to one human year. Most are in school until they are able to work in the mines or craft in an area of expertise such as jewelry or metal work. We're passing one of the guilds now. That would be for metal work such as forging tools like hammers and nails."

I look to my right to see an opening in the cave wall, decorated with glyphic writing. Dwarves scurry in and out of an opening where torchlight spills into the passage.

"Not much to see on the outside I guess."

"No. Not a glamorous life being a dwarf. But steady work." Carlsson turns around after a brief stop to watch the traffic from the cave. "It's good to see things are busy within the guild today. It means more orders must have come in from the surface."

"Who orders from the dwarves?" flows out of my mouth before I could stop it. Who knew this secret world of commerce existed?

"A lot of fairy kingdoms rely on the help of the dwarves to maintain their tools and items for homes. We are the expert metal workers for most things. Sometimes, you have to call in the experts."

Carlsson gives me a wink before he dashes off across the square. I follow him to head down another stone staircase. I look behind to see Brewford padding behind me. He doesn't seem winded by the speed we are going. But he is a mysterious 863-year-old cat. Who knows what could tire him out?

The traffic starts to ease off as we enter into what seems like the bottom of the cavern. Now, stone structures start to spire upward. Carvings of different animals and plants appear in the walls and arches as we pass. There are no crystals poking out at me. Instead, they are mounted in decorative places on the walls and in the carvings, glittering at me from torches hung for lighting. It seems like the city on the lower levels is bejeweled with stones.

We've entered the inner city. Finally. Brewford's head voice sounds impatient.

"What's wrong, Brewford?" I stop as he pads along behind me.

So much mining has led to endless corridors. Much harder to navigate the city this way. But dwarves never listen to advice.

He continues on, and I trail behind. I start to notice some of the stones mounted in decoration.

"Are all these real crystals? Some look as red as rubies." I stop to look at an especially green stone inlaid as leaves among stem carvings.

Brewford answers as I look at the stones. *Yes, these are different stones mined here abouts the Dwarf Kingdom. Rubies, emeralds, sapphires, as well as jet, onyx, and quartz crystals are used a lot in decorations in the city. Some of the less valuable stones are mined and traded in the fairy kingdoms. Come now, or we will lose the dwarf.*

I look up in time to see Carlsson turn onto a grand avenue lined with stone-faced buildings. We follow. The buildings are of a brown stone but inlaid with lighter stones for decorations. It is breathtaking to see the master carvings that decorate the buildings. The colors of red and green wink out of recesses of carvings, highlighting the scrollwork. Then, I look down the avenue and see it.

The Dwarf King's castle towers up toward the cavern ceiling with carved spires winking with jewels. Crystals and stones of all colors glitter around the surface. A variety of carved animals cover the surface. Bears are frozen in their growls. Snakes and lizards pose on vines and tree limbs. Doves and larks circle in lazy spirals frozen in stone. I can't imagine there is anything else quite like it, but it's especially awe-inspiring when seeing it for the first time.

"The king awaits within." Carlsson directs me forward, motioning me to walk with him. Not realizing I had stopped, I start to move ahead again.

You can close your mouth, too. Brewford's head voice chuckles.

I close it quickly. The pink I can feel spreading on my cheeks. But maybe, others did this mouth-gaping thing the first time they saw the castle.

Breathtaking the first time. I don't think they've needed to add much in the last three hundred years. But I'll tell you; it was five hundred years of waiting until this point. It was worth it, I think. Brewford strolls past and takes up the lead. I scamper behind as Carlsson follows me to the gate entrance.

We enter a hall draped in large tapestries depicting dwarves in battle. Dragons flame as dwarves hide behind shields. I study the walls as we pass.

"Some of these tapestries were made hundreds of years ago. They preserve the Dwarven history." Carlsson points at a particular tapestry, ragged around the edges. "This is one of the earlier tales; William the Good battling the large green dragon, Mrytar. Later, they were the first to come to a compromise and became allies. Future treaties were based on their first agreement." He shook his head. "And to think it was all over the right to mine different roots of the caves. Dwarves wanted to mine where the dragons wanted to live in peace. The compromise to share them has saved both races."

"What about that one?" I point to the fierce red dragon fighting another dwarf.

"Yes, Benedict the Fierce battling the Red Dragon King, Theldar. It was the final battle. It ended the war with the dragon race for centuries. Dragons returned to the Realm of Time and have been functioning as the time pathway heralds. Some of our caves are shared with them. We mine and they guard the entrances to the Realm of Time."

"Time? How did dragons turn into time pathway heralds?"

I hear the scratch of Brewford's nails upon the cobble stone floor. *It is a long story, for it was a long war. The dragons became the keepers of time to safe guard it. The dwarves share their caves to help them protect the secret. Sometimes, you can see the dragonfire used in forging with the dwarves. The compromise of dragonfire for forging and the added protection of the dwarves to safe guard the caves. In return, the dwarves gained the passage to mine in the Dragon Caves. It has been a good compromise for both races.*

"How do you know this, Brewford?" I accent the question with my hands on my hips.

I helped write the treaty, Wanda. He turns away before he can see my look of shock. I'm glad of that. We continue down the corridor, passing more tapestries. I look less at them now, still mulling over the fact that my cat could be a negotiator between dragons and dwarves. What else has he done in the last eight hundred years?

We enter the next hallway where several different flags hang about the walls. There is a unicorn-decorated flag, and a crowned fairy proudly displayed on another. Another flag has a dragon sitting on top of a mountain. Its tail wraps around a sword as it breathes fire. I don't have much time to look at all the flags, for we turn left into a side room.

The steward dwarf steps into the doorway. "His Majesty has asked for you to wait for him here. He will arrive shortly for an audience. Master Carlsson." The steward does a formal head bob in his direction. Then, he turns and bows toward my cat. "Sorcerer Brewford, it is good to see you again."

"As well as to see you Head Steward Alster." Brewford returns the nod. The steward backs out of the room, closing the double doors behind him.

I can only stand the silence for about a minute. "So now what? We just sit here?"

"Royalty cannot be rushed, Keeper Wanda." Carlsson sits down and folds his arms. "We wait."

I guess there is no Internet connection down here. So I know there aren't any video games or computers hidden behind curtains. There aren't even books on the shelves.

The art of waiting is not something I've had a lot of practice in. So, I look around for something to do. There isn't much in the room, but large billowy curtains of dark green velvet. I try to see if there is something to look at. Luckily there is a hidden alcove behind the curtain that contains a vase standing on a small marble shelf built into the wall. Veins of marble run through the shelf, and I start to trace them. The vase is empty. It looks like the Greek museum pieces I've seen on-line.

I let the curtain fall back. The other walls are decorated with more tapestries. They have scenes of woods and forests. Some have mysterious creatures that stare back. I'm having a staring contest with a bear when the double doors open.

Carlsson rushes to his feet and bows. A heavyset dwarf stands in the doorway. He has on a purple velvet cap with a long point that bends and runs down to the floor. It's much longer than Carlsson's hat. He has on what looks like a jerkin, leather, and rings set into the flaps. He has leather pants and sturdy boots. His beard is grey and drags along the floor. If it gets much longer, I'm sure he'll be stepping on it as he walks. His nose is bigger than Carlsson's. His eyes gaze kindly as they turn toward me. A brilliant green sparkles from within them, and I can tell this has got to be the king. He stands upright with a lot of confidence. I could definitely take lessons from him on how to look self-assured.

"Who visits asking the help of the dwarves? Human child, is it you?" He extends his pointer finger to motion me forward. "If it is you, be quick. I have much to do today."

Again, all the lessons from my Renaissance Fair visits come back to me. I bow slightly. "Your Majesty." He nods to me before I continue. "I am a Crystal Keeper from the Western Realm. I do have need of a new crystal. You see, my little brother got it off my nightstand and started swinging it. He ran and whacked it in the hall . . ."

"Enough human child. Helping a Crystal Keeper is a duty the dwarves hold dear. You keep the realms safe and assist us when you can." He stops and pulls his beard for a moment. "What ever you need, it shall be granted. As it is, we could use the help of a Crystal Keeper as well. I would like to ask for your assistance with a grave issue."

"I'm guessing it's the imbalance within the . . ." I wanted to say Force, but I don't think that he's ever heard of Star Wars. So I catch myself and end with ". . . fairy paths. Brewford and my Unicorn guide sensed it while traveling to the Dwarven Kingdom."

"Brewford? I haven't heard that name mentioned in a century, at least." The king looks down at Brewford standing just a few feet from me. He's sitting in his normal cat stance with his eyes half closed.

He nods toward the king. *It's a pleasure to meet with Your Majesty again. The balance has been upset. I can sense a draw of energy somewhere on the paths, but I cannot be sure of the source. I do believe that it must be traced.*

"It is how I feared. We, too, could sense it out of balance. But we do not travel the paths as often as other fairy folk. We prefer our mines. Our treaty with the dragons allows some travel on the time pathways, which come in handy for deliveries. They're always on time." He smiles at this and turns to me.

"So, Keeper, what would you suggest? We can equip you with a new crystal of your choice, and then will you help us?"

I don't know how this happens. More problems drop in my lap. By now, I was seeing how the way of a Keeper often leads you from one problem to the next. Problems seem to be interconnected. But, Keepers help the fairy folk. That's our job.

Besides, I was curious about all the talk about dragons. Were they like my dream? Terrifying and belching flame is the only picture I had of them so far. I have to admit, I was curious to meet one. But then, my dream keeps creeping back in my mind. Running. Running. Flames at my back. It can't be a coincidence. Maybe my dream was a warning.

"Dragons, are they friendly?" There, I was facing the fear of my dream finally. I looked expectantly at the king.

"Do they worry you, Keeper? Dragons, I must say, are very elusive. We hardly see them unless they are at the forges lending their dragonfire to make magical items. They help guide dwarf artisans or masters to make deliveries. But other than that, they do keep to themselves. I would say they are very friendly, if you don't anger them first."

I sigh deeply. "Well, I was just not sure since where I come from, dragons can be pretty nasty, with burning down villages and all. At least, that is what's said about them in stories."

The king laughs shaking his full belly. I start to blush. This wasn't going well, and I don't really like being laughed at. I shift from one foot to the other until he stops.

"Wanda, you surface dwellers really are out of touch with the World of Fairy. Only your tales of old remain, and they are not very accurate. Things get lost in the telling of a story. Embellishments make stories more dramatic. There is truth between the lines."

He chuckles again before continuing. "Besides, the wars with the dragons did portray them as an enemy for a while.

Now, of course, all is well with the treaty. The keeping of peace is important."

"But let us move onto more important issues." He moves to a large chair against the wall. He motions to a bench across from him. I sit. Brewford jumps up and sits next to me. The Brew sits tall, with his tail swishing from side to side.

I feel comforted finding out that dragons were on the side of good. I guess the dream might just be a dream. "I just had some reservations about dragons. That's all. If I'm going to help, I just like to be careful. I'd hate to be on the paths and run into an unfriendly dragon."

The Dwarf King nods leaning on his elbow. "So, Keeper child, can you help find the source of the imbalance?"

I don't answer at first. Could I do this? Travel the paths and make it to the source of drainage? I'd need help for sure. "I think I can, if I have the help of some friends." I look down at Brewford. "Will you come, Brew?"

With a flick of his tail, he starts to settle into a large fur ball on the bench. His eyes grow half closed. *Of course, Keeper Wanda.* Oh, he'd gotten formal. This must be serious. *But I think we need a master guide. The drain could be on the time pathways as well as the fairy paths. We must not leave out any options to explore.*

"Done." The Dwarf King starts to stroke his beard. "I think I know who would be a wonderful guide for this endeavor. Let us get you fitted with a new crystal. And then, it's off to the paths."

Something gnaws at the back of my mind. School. How much was I missing? Mom would kill me if my grades went down because I was on Keeper business. "There is one more thing. I have an English test coming up Friday. I might need time to study before. I can't miss too much time in the Real World."

Do not worry, Wanda. Brewford purrs with confidence. *I think we'll have all the time we need in the world.*

CHAPTER 7

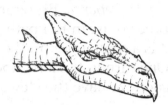

New Friends

We walk out of the castle through a series of tunnels. They don't have any crystals. Just a lot of dirt, but warmth emanates from the walls. I follow behind Dwarf Carlsson, Brewford next to me, and the steward from the castle is in the lead, carrying a torch, taking us down a sloping path. The torch sputters and smokes, giving off the smell of burned wood. I love that smell. It always reminds me of camping with my dad during the time before the divorce. Before my brother was around.

The path curves around, and we head down a steep set of stairs. Brewford has to hop down to keep up. Then, we head toward a door that the steward knocks on with a steady rhythm. Thump, thump. Thump. It swings open with a swish, and we head through.

It turns out to be a rather nice passage, lined with torches. The dirt walls are reinforced with beams of wood, like I'd seen in pictures of old Western mines. As we continue down the path, rocks start to form the walls until the dirt is replaced entirely of rock. Within the rock shine different sparkles of gold. Interwoven with white rock are veins of gold, glinting in the light of the torches. The veins move up in different patterns, creating a marble wall effect. I tear myself away from the patterns in time to see Carlsson turn down a left fork in the path, followed by the steward.

"Where are we going?" I whisper to Brewford.

You need to watch your worrying, Wanda. Sometimes it is good to follow the flow of events. Patience. Brewford pads forward to lead me around another twist in the path. The crunch of the dirt beneath my feet is a companion to the progress we make down the passage. One turn to the left. Another to the right. I keep thinking, it's good we have the steward to lead us. I am completely lost.

Finally, we come to an abrupt stop. It is another door, lit by torches on both sides. It has amazing gold work decorating the hinges and front. Scrolled decorations surround the doorknob that sticks out as a lip to the door.

The steward knocks again. This time the knocks were a bit more complicated. Thump, thump. Small thump, large thump. Thump. Bang. The door slowly opens and a dwarf peeks his head out. "What is it? Who disturbs the Guild of Crystals?"

"The king has ordered that this Human Keeper be issued a new crystal," the steward announces.

"As the king wishes." The door dwarf nods and motions us through.

"If you be wishing a crystal, head down the passage and turn right. The crystal room will have someone on duty to help you. I shall lead you to the crystal room. Follow me."

"Thank you," I answer. It seems the polite thing to say; considering it's my crystal we're after.

Dwarves look up from their work as we pass. They nod to the door dwarf as we walk down the corridor. The passage is lined with clear quartz crystal. Points thrust in different directions. The crystals are not numerous on this path, but still dangerous if you weren't paying attention to where the crystals angled outward.

We arrive at another door at the end of the hall. This one is of solid white quartz. It is polished to a shine like a giant, tumbled stone, except it's a door. I'm not sure how this one will open since it hasn't any doorknob. But the door dwarf doesn't hesitate with his pounding knocks. This time there are four. Thump. Thump. Thump. Thump. Each time he knocks, the door reverberates the sound. He turns and leaves before there is an answer.

We wait a bit until another dwarf pokes his head around the door. "What is it?" He sounds very gruff and annoyed at being disturbed. "I've got more crystals to cut before day's end. This better be good."

"If you would pardon us, Master Cutter Larson," answers the steward. "The king wishes to have this Human Keeper outfitted with another crystal pendant."

"It is of great importance, Master Larson," interrupted Carlsson. "Her other pendant has been damaged, and the fairy within is in pain. She needs to be transferred as soon as possible."

"Humph," Master Larson grunts back. "Fine. That is a worthy reason to interrupt my work. Please enter." The door swings back into the wall leaving a passage completely carved out of crystal. In fact, the whole room is a chamber of white quartz. The floor has a slight scuff to it so we won't slip.

Master Larson directs me to a place to sit on some wooden benches set into the walls. Crystal curves over them forming an alcove. "Sit. This may take some time." He heads over to his workbench, a large wooden table of dark wood. I look at the sheer beauty. Candlelight is absorbed in the crystal walls as if backlighting them. It's like being in a rainbow chamber.

Before I get comfortable, he motions to me. "Come here, Keeper." Master Larson waves me to his workbench. I walk over and find a stool set next to the workbench. It wobbles a bit when I hop on. I have to grab the side of the table to steady myself.

Crystal shards are on top of the table scattered randomly about. Master Larson reaches up to some pendants hanging from a wooden shelf. They're hanging by hooks. Each one has masterful decorations. Some have wire wrapping of gold, some silver work swirling about the top. I see leaves and stones woven around each crystal. There are so many different designs; it's hard to focus on just one.

"Choose carefully. It will be a choice to last a lifetime."

"How do I know which one?"

"You'll know it when you see it. Let your hand drift over them. See which one feels right."

I reach toward the crystals hanging on the shelf. I start touching each one to see if I feel something special. I touch one, then another. I feel the smooth metal wrapped around one. Then, I run my finger over a smooth, metal cap of another. But none of them feels right.

Wait. I notice a crystal lying on the bench. It has a bluish color with a rainbow effect to the facets. That one. It feels perfect. It feels slightly warm and tingles. I pick it up and feel an instant surge to my temples. It grows warmer in my hand. "This one." I hold it up to the master cutter.

He strokes his grey beard and reaches for it. He holds it in his fingers and twirls it to get a good look at all sides. "Wise choice, Keeper. This is a rare crystal, infused with rainbow essence. It's very good at drawing and holding energy. Should be useful for you and a good home for your crystal fairy." He puts it down on the table. "If I could have your current crystal pendant. I will start work on it immediately."

I pull the leather cord that holds my pendant over my head and hand it to the dwarf. He looks it over, turning it side to side. He ends with a grumph. "No wonder it broke. It has a defect in the side of the crystal, here." He points to a place in the middle of the point. "Good thing it cracked now. Your fairy can be safely transferred. Had it gotten worse, she might have been unable to leave. Crystal fairies are touchy sorts. They need the right crystal to live within."

"It won't hurt her to leave and go to a new crystal?"

He laughs at my question. Very loud. What was it with dwarves that makes them laugh so loud?

"No, Keeper. In fact, the new crystal will help her more. It's a better point for her, really. More room and energy for her to draw on. Now, leave me." He motions me from the bench. "Return in three bells and your crystal fairy will have a new home."

"Bells?"

"Time is measured by a bell ringing," mentions Carlsson. He starts to shuffle off the bench. "With no sun here, hours are measured by the ringing of a bell at each turn of the hour."

"Oh. Makes sense, I guess." I slip off the stool. Looking around, I ask, "What do we do now?"

"I think it's time to meet your guide," suggests the steward. "Thank you, Master Larson."

"Humph." He doesn't even look back at us from his workbench. He continues to work, sitting on the stool at his workbench as we go out the crystal door.

The darkness seems endless as we leave the brightness of the crystal chamber. Warmth again emanates from the walls and a halo of light circles us as we travel along the passageway. I'm not sure how, but Brewford seems to give his tail a twitch to the left. And then, a bang, and a ball of light. Who am I to question the ways of a cat sorcerer?

"Good timing with the ball of light, Brew."

A beginner's spell, Wanda. I think it is time to put it on your instruction list.

"Cool. That's something that will be cool to know."

We continue down the path. Smoky quartz points wedge outward from the walls. Their glint shows me the edges of the dark passage. In spite of the darkness and only one ball of light, it feels almost cozy. The bumps of the dark crystals seem to insulate sounds as our feet scuff along in the dirt.

After a time, we reach the end of the passage. Or so it seems. I reach out to touch the wall in front of us. It's all black stone. I touch the smooth surface, with a slight reflection. It reminds me of obsidian, like the stone Native Americans used for arrowheads.

"Now what do we do?" I wonder out loud. No one seems to offer an answer. So I ask again, "Do we just stand here and wait?"

"Actually, yes." The steward takes a torch from its holder on the wall. I hear the creak of metal. The ball of light starts to fade. The steward continues, "We wait until asked to enter. It would be rude to do otherwise." The whole place starts to seem glum when only lit by one torch.

"Oh, great." I fold my arms. For a kid, I usually have a lot of patience. You do what adults tell you, most of the time. But if it takes too long, I always try to think of another way. "You sure that's all we can do?"

There is no answer. "Great." I start to look around at the walls, and see that it still looks like a bunch of dirt and crystals. But then I notice a rather dark red vein of something running along a lower part of the wall. I bend down for a better look. I trace it with my finger, following it as it leads toward the stone door. "This is kinda cool. It's a really dark red while the rest is black."

I feel along and push inward. Suddenly, the stone door slides back into the wall, and a rush of air draws us inward.

"Who goes there?" From within, a booming voice answers.

"Oh, now you've gone and done it, Keeper. He doesn't like to be disturbed until he's ready." The steward twists his hands together. "I suggest we take this slowly, as to not disrespect the Great Firekeeper."

"Well, we've already disturbed him. I'll just go in and explain." I enter, ducking my head under the curve of the upper doorway.

Wanda, I wouldn't do that, I hear Brewford's mind speech too late.

I only have enough time to stop before the terrible roar.

CHAPTER 8

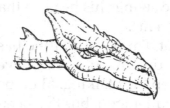

Sydney

The first roar is bad enough. It is followed by an equally terrifying growl. Then, a booming voice says, "Who disturbs the Great Fire Keeper as he rests after his long shift at the mines?"

Well, I'd already stepped into things this far. I better finish. I ease forward. "That would be me, great booming voice. I'm sorry to disturb you, but I'm on Crystal Keeper business looking for my guide. If you happen to know . . ."

A large shape turns the corner, and I see him for the first time. For some reason, I thought a dragon would be much bigger. But he is only just larger than a horse. But then, this is the first time I've seen a real dragon.

He lives up to my expectations in appearance at least. He has scaly dragon features, a ridge along his back, small wings pulled back at his sides, and a long lizard tail. He looks like he has stepped out of a bad version of Jurassic Park. His skin has a faint luminous glow that lights the cave slightly. This gives a pearl effect to his red-orange skin. His golden eyes are looking at me, and a puff of smoke coming out of his nostrils every time he breathes. He definitely has a Komodo Dragon beat.

"Yes," he answers in human words. There are no telepath words to my mind. That was surprising, too. His lips articulated the human words with a slight lisp. "I do admire your bravery so far. Usually that answer scares away anyone that bothers me. So, you wanted my attention, Human Child. What is it then?" He swings his head so that one of his yellow eyes focuses right on me.

I clear my throat. I'm not sure if he has many teeth. I try not to think of my dream. At least, I have a little control of the situation if I keep him talking. "I do beg your pardon for the intrusion, Friend Dragon, but I've been told that I need a guide to help check the paths for an imbalance in the flow of energies. Do you know of one?"

His laughter feels like a hot wind. "How long have you been a Crystal Keeper, young human?"

I creep closer to the wall of the cave. It is sandy, and crumbles off as my back leans against it. "Almost half a year." I hold up my chin, realizing I might look braver if I ease away from the wall.

The dragon snuffles his laughter and snorts. "I thought so. Only a new Keeper would walk so fearlessly into danger. Caution, I think, is something you should practice in the future, human."

I inch further away from the wall. "You can call me Wanda, you know."

"Wanda, then." He hobbles over toward me, lowering his head to my level. "I am the guide you seek, Wanda. I am, as you say, a type of guide for the paths."

"Okay, Dragon. If you're my guide, I'm sure I'll need to call you something."

His name is Sydney. Brewford's voice echoes in my mind as I feel a whoosh of fur go past my legs. *And he is the best Fire Forger in the Dwarven Lands.*

The dragon chuckles. "Brewford, my favorite feline sorcerer. I see your fur has grown back."

Brewford lets out a "humph" as he jumps onto a nearby rock ledge. Some of the stones slide off as he adjusts to better footing. The dwarves come in and bow their heads to the ground. Each takes a turn bobbing up and down, until they look like they are doing some sort of dance.

"Rise, I acknowledge you, good dwarves. Thank you for bringing these lost outside souls. I will show them the way they seek." His voice seems less booming and more kind as he nods to the dwarves.

"Thank you, Sydney the Great. We will let the king know of your help in this matter."

Each does a quick bow again. The steward turns the corner, and we can hear his steps retreating down the corridor. Carlsson comes over and shakes my hand. "Goodbye, Keeper. May you find what you need along the paths. Travel safely."

"Thank you, Carlsson. I don't think I would have found my way in the city without you."

He bows to me, to Brewford, and last to the dragon. Backing out, he turns and leaves us in the chalk cave with the dragon. I glance around at the walls as Carlsson leaves. I notice inlaid shells, some of them with an opalescent gleam. It is like looking at an ocean under the ground.

"Used to be an underwater lake here, back when land was up higher. But it's been pulled lower by the movement of the land above." The dragon now has an older gentleman's voice, clear and to the point. "We had better get going. You'll have time to explore later. But you're welcome to take one of the shells with you. They are great for magnifying creativity when you need it. Plus, a shell represents home. If you have a shell with you, home is always within."

I look at the wall and move closer. I walk along to feel the curves. The shells are all sticking out in different directions. I can only see a bit of each one. I see a brown shell with a bit of a swirl on the edge. It has what looks like brown and white stripes on the edge. "I choose this one." As I say it, the sand starts to fall away, and it is easy for me to pull it out of the wall. Chalky sand falls around my feet. The shell is smooth with flashes of opal.

"It's a opalized fossil, Wanda. Most are in this section of the mines." The dragon responds to my look toward him. "See there, if you turn it, you can see where parts of the shell have turned to opal. The one you picked has got some real fire in it."

I look at the shell and see flashes of red and green along the edge. The beginning of the shell curls into its center, looking like your average garden snail shell. It is beautiful. I trace the spiral with my finger.

"Careful, Keeper, you'll get lost in the comforts of home. Got to keep your mind moving to be free. But it is a nice thing to have that feeling of assurance. Tracing the shell's spiral can be comforting, especially when facing terrible odds."

I watched the flashes of blue, green, and red in the spaces of opal. "I definitely do that a lot. This could come in handy. I've come across other things that have helped in the Fairy World. Thank you, Dragon." I place it in the front pocket of my jeans.

"Call me Sydney." His lips spread into a smile. "I think it's always best to know friends on a first-name basis."

"Sydney then. Glad to meet you. Sorry I rushed in and startled you."

"All is well. You didn't know there was a dragon sitting about. I'd scare my own sister if she didn't know I was there. Of course, sometimes it is fun to scare your little sister or brother to keep them from sneaking up and bothering you. But you always have to remember one important fact."

"And that is," I look at Sydney for a bit. Waiting.

He snorts a puff of smoke. "They get bigger." He starts a big turn. "Come. We've got some fairy paths to investigate." He lumbers off toward the back of his cave. I start to follow after, with Brewford close behind me. There is a burst of air in the tunnel. The air is thicker. Suddenly, the corridor starts to glow.

The walls continue to have shells of all sorts wedged in at different angles. Some of the layers change colors as we go deeper. The fairy path is lined with torches. I can see some of the shades of white chalk change to a reddish brown. Below are layers of orange and a dark brown. It looks like cliffs on the edge of the ocean.

"How do we start, Sydney? I've got to be back to pick up my crystal pendant later from the master cutter. Is it going to take long?"

"Children always want to rush things." The dragon snorts. "Patience, Wanda. A mystery is never solved quickly, but with patience and a keen sense of observation, you can find the clues."

Oh, I'm getting the feeling that this dragon loves to give lectures more than Brewford. I follow him as he lumbers down the passage. The shells continue to be embedded in the walls around me, but the sandy color is getting darker. Every once in a while, Sydney gives a flap to his wings. They extend outward from his body a few inches and stretch. Then, he folds them tight along his body again. It's like when you stretch your arms while sitting at a desk for a long time.

We finally arrive at a fork in the pathways. One turns left while the other goes right. Down one is a faint glow of blue. Down the other passage is a faint glow of green.

"Now what?" I ask while putting my hands on my hips. The shells have disappeared completely. There isn't much to see down either path. I am wondering what is making the passages glow.

"This is where you choose the correct path, Keeper." The dragon answers in a rumbling voice. "Which will be the path you choose?"

"There's not much to go on here." I try to peer left, then right. All I can see is the glow. "The only difference that I can see is that one is blue and the other is green."

"Good. You're observing details, and not rushing into a decision." There is a rumble of approval, followed by a reptilian smile.

"Which would you choose, Brewford," I say looking around for a tabby backside.

It's your choice to make, Wanda. You're the Keeper in this quest.

"What makes my choice so important?"

There is a chuckle from the dragon before he answers. "Sometimes making a choice is half the problem solved. You've noted one is blue and one is green. What else can you observe to help you make a decision?"

Hmmm. I squint and look at each opening carefully. "The green passage seems to be brighter than the blue passage."

Good, what else? Brewford answers in his head voice.

I feel a breeze coming out of the green passage. There is no chill to the blue passage. "I think the green passage is cooler. It has a breeze in it. Maybe it leads down."

"Anything more?" The dragon sways his head a bit closer to me.

"That's it, I think." I shrug my shoulders.

"That's a good start with observations," Sydney's voice sounded supportive. "Now, can they help you make a choice?"

I look at one passage and then the other. "I'd like to try to stay warm, but want to be able to see well. I wonder if the color of the pathway has some significance to where it goes?"

I knew we'd have a breakthrough here. Brewford's head voice struck a chord as he said it.

"Yes, Master Cat Sorcerer, it seems our Keeper is starting to realize she can ask questions to get at an answer."

"But I already know how to ask questions," I plead with a bit more nasal in my voice than I'd like.

"Yes, but not the right ones," answered Brewford.

"Have you made a choice?" asked Sydney.

"I don't know. It would help if I knew where we needed to go to find the leak in the path balances."

"I was hoping you could tell us, Keeper. After all, you might be able to feel it as well."

"Feel it? Like feeling the 'force' or something? That's super Jedi Knight."

"Comparing a Crystal Keeper to a knight is not far off, Wanda," Brewford said. "But yes, your Keeper abilities should allow you too feel something out of balance on the paths. Give it a try. See if something feels wrong to you about one of the paths."

I move closer to the blue passageway. I reach toward the wall where the opening connects with our passageway. It is smooth and cool, almost like glass. A pulse of blue light moves away down the corridor from me. It has the feeling of purpose to it.

"I don't think there is anything wrong with this path. It seems to have things moving along in it okay."

"Try the next one," directs Sydney. He moves his tail aside so I can move to the other side of our sandy passage. I reach and put my hand on the green corridor wall. This time it hums an off-chord tune. There is a flash under my hand and a shock wave goes through it. It knocks me flat on my butt like an electric shock.

"Wow, there is definitely something wrong here!" I get up and brush myself off.

"Then, we've found the right passage to investigate," announces Sydney. "Come, let us see where the leak may be."

CHAPTER 9

Promises, Promises

We head into the green passageway. I immediately don't like this fairy path at all. It is strewn with black rocks that crunch under my feet. The whole place is lit up by the glowing green walls that have an unsteady flashing rhythm. It is a pulsing strobe that makes me shield my eyes as we walk.

"Boy, this doesn't feel right. What could be wrong, Brew?" I cover my eyes as I look down for Brewford.

He is scampering along dodging around some large rocks that are along the edge of the walkway. *There is a definite imbalance on this fairy path. It seems to connect to a lot of other paths. It could be unsettling them. I suggest we stick to the center. It will be easier to avoid energy surges.*

"Energy what?" I ask.

He stops to look back at me. I almost stumble over the top of him. He sits down, closing his eyes half way. *Energy surges are the bursts of energy that feed into the fairy paths. Most paths are balanced, so their energy tends to hum at a static rate. This path is very out of tune. Surges could throw the whole path off center.*

At that moment a rumbling starts at the far end of the path.

"Like right now. I suggest we take cover," says Sydney.

Hit the dirt, Wanda! Brewford's mind shout prompts quick action. Sydney lowers himself down onto the path as I throw myself onto the gravel. I eat a bit of dust and scrape my chin before the first shock wave hits.

A rolling wave in the floor flows underneath me. It bobs me up and down until the last few rolls ripple to stillness. Dang. It was like being in an earthquake or riding a roller coaster, except we were not in a car with a safety strap. I'm happy I am able to get close to the ground. I have a feeling this would have knocked me on my butt if I'd been standing.

I wait for the rolling to stop. Then, a few seconds later, I stand up brushing off the black gravel. Some of it sticks to my hand. Luckily, I only have some scratches on my palms and probably my chin. My knees are not thrashed due to the fact I'm wearing jeans.

"Are you okay, Keeper?" Sydney asks.

"Yeah, I think so." I rub my hands together to knock off the rest of the gravel.

I glance at the walls as I finish wiping the rest of the gravel from my jeans. First, I see a reflection of myself that swirls away. Then, I see the cave that Eddie disappeared in. There I am, standing, watching Balkazaar grab her and run back through the portal. I see myself scream, but with no sound.

Both land with Balkazaar still firmly gripping her around the waist. She is hitting him with both arms, but he seems to ignore it. Then, he swings her around and motions for someone to come forward. It is another Eddie. Everything about her is the same, the clothes, her hair, shoes, eyes, and even her pendant. The only difference is that the other Eddie wears a scowl that turns into a horrible grin when Balkazaar motions toward the portal. This other Eddie enters the portal while Balkazaar pushes the real Eddie forward. They look like they are in a field of grass, with rose bushes. Around the edge it looks like my school's walkways. Then, all goes blurry. And I see my reflection again. That's when the next rumble starts.

"Here comes another one," I shout shaking off the scene I'd seen in the wall. This time I slide sideways instead of face forward. I eat less gravel. The rolling action rumbles onward through the path lasting a little longer than the first time.

I get up and brush myself off again. "Maybe it's getting worse. That one was bigger than the last."

Or the energy can sense we're coming. Whatever is causing the leak might know we're here. Brewford sounds more serious than usual. He looks tense standing with his tail out, whipping it back and forth, looking alert for another rolling wave.

I watch the dragon lumber ahead. "Can we get to the leak before the next wave hits, Sydney?"

There is a rumble in the distance before Sydney answers, "Yes, if we hurry, Wanda."

I don't get a chance to tell them what I've seen yet. I figure we better get to where the energy leak is before more shock waves roll through the passage. We step up our pace.

Sydney is a bit clunkier than a unicorn. He walks more like an elephant; all four legs lumbering to get him down the passage. But he has one advantage. He has a longer stride than both of us. Brewford pads along at a cat jog. I start doing my power walking I'd learned from P.E.

The green pulses of light continue in the walls. The rumbles warn us of another shock wave, and we duck onto the gravel floor until it passes. I get into a rhythm of walk, slide, sit, and walk again.

Finally, there is a noticeable flicker in the walls to the left. A passage branches off there, and the walls down that direction are flashing on and off like a fluorescent light about ready to go out.

"This way." I point down the flickering green corridor. As we turn down it, the flickering stops on all sides. The passage starts to dim as we continue down. The gravel crunches under my feet. There is a steady flashing as we continue our fast pace. Finally, the corridor almost dims completely. I don't need to shield my eyes anymore. It's like all the energy in this particular path is almost gone. And then I can hear it. There is an off key hum, like when a refrigerator needs fixing.

We get closer. The hum starts to sound like all the keys played on the piano at once, over and over. I have to put my hands over my ears before saying, "I think we found it. That sounds awful." I look at a space in the wall that seems to be playing the chord. A black vortex swirls where all the green light enters it. Nothing comes out of the black space. All of the green flashes of light are swirling right into it.

Brewford's whiskers bristle. *We've got to close it.*

"How?" I let the question hang in the air as I look to Brewford, then Sydney.

"Wanda, do you still have your shell from my cave?"

"Yes, but how will that help?"

"I told you that shells represent home. If we were to send the energy entering the vortex home, it might seal it."

"Okay. But how do I do that?"

"Just think of home, Wanda," says Sydney gently.

I laugh. I can't help it. "You're acting way too much like the Good Witch of the South."

Brewford interrupts my giggle. *Wanda, try to redirect your thoughts and go for the Dorothy angle. Really, you do need to think of home.*

I smile and start a chant I can't resist. "There's no place like home. There's no place like home." I start giggling again. I cover my mouth, but it starts into a full-blown laugh. "Really, I don't think I can."

"No, not you going home, but the energy returning home." Sydney says as if he was a teacher correcting me in school.

Please, Wanda, show some decorum. Brewford gives me a half-eye-closed stare. He adjusts sitting on the gravel. It must be uncomfortable for a cat. *Maybe the phone home thing isn't working. Try thinking reset like in one of your human video games.*

"Okay, that helps a bit more." The laughter seems to stop bubbling up after that. I think of pushing restart on my video system. It's an old PS2 system. Not flashy, but it plays games. I keep thinking, start over, and go home. I hold the shell in my hands and keep imagining pushing that reset button.

"Okay, now slowly place the shell in the center of the vortex." Sydney says directing my next step.

I open my eyes and slowly stand up. I lean against the wall just above the vortex. There is a shudder underneath my hand. A lot of flashing green light speeds beneath my hand entering into the vortex.

"Reset Now," I shout as I shove the shell into the center. It gets slurped up as if dropping into a pond. Then, the shell settles in and spins around in a circle. It is like it is on the other side of a glass wall. It spins and stops. The opalescent sides have energy flashing along its edge. The black begins to fade. Slowly, starting from the shell, the black is replaced by a faint green that grows stronger and stronger. The shuddering in the floor stops.

"I believe you've done well, Keeper. This breach in the balance seems healed." Sydney nudges his head against my side. I instinctively start rubbing his eye ridge. I'd always wanted a lizard as a pet. Lizard, dragon, whatever. There doesn't seem to be much difference right now. He lifts his head up a bit, and I give him a good scratch under his chin.

"At least this one seems to be taken care of. I can sense other imbalances along the pathways. Not nearby, but with other sources that may have a black vortex such as this." Brewford adds with his half-eye stare.

"Then I believe it is time to hold council. We need to see how many of these are about the paths causing the imbalance," agrees Sydney, stopping his lean upward to be scratched.

"Yeah, and boy do I have something to tell you guys."

"Yes, friend Keeper, what is it?" The dragon says looking eye to eye with me.

"I saw Balkazaar in the walls as we were having one of those rolling tremors."

"Indeed." His golden eyes fix on me. "Come. We will return to the Dwarven Kingdom and alert the king. He will need to let the other Fairy Rulers know of this change of fortune. Time is of the essence."

"Whenever Balkazaar is involved, being fortunate is always a good thing to remember," reminds Brewford. He nods down the path. "After you, Dragon Sydney."

CHAPTER 10

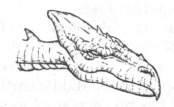

A Meeting of the Minds

It is a little like déjà vu. Elves sitting around a big crystal table, seated in crystal chairs, wearing long flowing robes. Definitely a *Lord of the Rings* scene. What is different is the dwarves are at this meeting along with some Fairy Queens I know already, and ones I don't know. Oh yeah, and the table is much bigger this time.

It wasn't a hard journey back to the Dwarven castle. Sydney had talked to the king, and within what seemed like an hour, elves and fairies descended into the great halls. A bell sounded, and we scuttled into the great crystal chamber. It seems each kingdom has a chamber like this. Of course.

Lillith, the Queen of the West, also my personal mentor queen, is in attendance at the council as well as Eddie's queen, the tree sprite, Queen Alira. The Elven Elder Geldon is to her left, and the Dwarf King is next to him. Other faces circle the table dressed in flowing gowns and capes. Crystals are interwoven into the hair of the elves.

But there are fairy folk of other lands as well. A troll and an ogre represent the deep earth kingdoms. Sydney, seated on a cushion near the table, represents the dragons. But one fairy caught my eye.

Near the end of the table is a Hawaiian woman sitting with a white muu'muu. She has a head wreath of leaves and a lei of yellow flowers is about her neck. She has short black hair and slight wrinkles around her eyes.

The dwarves have crystals interwoven in their beards and hair. Several purple—and silver-haired elves are wearing silver hairpieces. It is like a fantasy fair with a lot of people doing their best impression of Middle Earth, but it's for real.

Even Brewford has his own stool to sit at the table. He peers over to look at me, slowly closing his eyes. He seems calm for something like this. But he always seems to know what's up. Even Master Castrotomas is seated next to him. It is definitely a big meeting.

I take another moment to just let the gentle banter of all the people around the table lull me. Sometimes it is scenes like this that make being a Crystal Keeper unbelievable. I sigh. Then I notice I am the only Keeper. Also, I'm the only human.

There is a tapping of a staff at the far end of the table. All heads turn toward the front table. A silver-haired elf stands and nods in all the directions around the table. "Good friends of the Fairy Realms, I welcome you to this Great Council. I wish we could meet under circumstances that were not of grave danger. It is how it is in the world. Great minds must gather to solve a problem. We gather at difficult times to find the solutions that will save our worlds. Today, we have such a gathering."

He takes a deep breath and closes his eyes before continuing. "Balkazaar is trying to return to the Real World." There are short gasps and raised voices. He waves his hand. "I know this is alarming news. But I am assured that he is not completely free. He has been making attempts that have been thwarted." He motions toward me. "We have one of the Keepers that helped stop one of his attempts seated with us now."

I hate it when everyone looks at me. When they sing "Happy Birthday" to you at a restaurant, half the time I want to sink into my chair. This is ten times worse. I'm not sure what to do. I do a kind of hand salute and smile. There are some nods and whispers.

I sink a little in my chair. Luckily, Geldon continues, "The paths are now imbalanced due to his attempts. There have been repairs to some of his damage. But it is going to have to be stopped at the source. We have to reseal his prison for good."

He waits for the surprised gasps to die down again before continuing. "It has been brought to my attention that a doppelganger has replaced one of the Keepers. Maybe Balkazaar is already onto us and is replacing them to gain the power he needs to break from his prison. It is a pattern that he has been gathering power when he can, only to be stopped by the brave Keeper among us now."

Again, all the heads swerve to eye me over. I'm sure I am blushing. But then, I have a moment. It comes to me in a quick thought. I blurt out, "But I still don't know where my friend Eddie is. She's a Keeper, too. She was the one replaced with a doppelganger. Maybe her disappearance is tied to all this."

"More than likely," Geldon says. "I think she is being used to help free Balkazaar. If he gets enough Keepers, he'll be able to free himself. We must counter his move somehow."

"How is he to be resealed?" asks Queen Alira, the tree sprite. "It took the Council of Twelve last time. How are we going to be able to entreat the help of that many Keepers?"

"There haven't been that many Crystal Keepers since the great wars," adds another elf down the table. "Where will we find that many? The humans have lost touch with us."

A burst of voices breaks out, forcing Geldon to tap his staff. Tap, tap, tap. Slowly, the talking subsides.

Geldon eyes everyone at the table before he starts. "But not their children. Sometimes children have a stronger power. They are filled with the possibilities of their lives, and not spoiled yet with the poisons of the world. We gather the

Crystal Keepers. The children that help us in both worlds. It will be a difficult task."

But we might have time on our side. Brewford's head voice rings in my head. Other faces turn toward him. He must be telepathically sending to the whole council. *We might be able to retrieve some Keepers from the past to help with the closure in the present.*

"Yes, Master Brewford is right." I recognize Master Castrotomas interrupting Brewford. He is the master cat sorcerer that helped me in Ireland. He continues, while pushing back his glasses with his paw. "If we are able to gather Crystal Keepers from the present and the points of the past that had strong numbers of Keepers, we might be able to gather enough."

"We will need some Keepers from the present to gather Keepers of the past. They will need to travel in time to gather them," adds Queen Lillith. She looks over to me with an encouraging look. Her grandmotherly smile makes me feel less nervous.

There is a knock on the great oak double doors to the hall. Geldon motions for the guard to open them. One of the dwarf guards turns and heads to the doors. Several elves turn their attention toward the entrance. Geldon adds, "Let us see what our new member of the council feels will work."

I have to turn a bit in my chair to see who is at the door. It is a boy. A human boy. He has black hair and blue eyes. He wears a T-shirt and zipped up hoodie with jeans. His tennis shoes squeak on the marble floor as he enters. Around his neck is a crystal pendant. I stop staring long enough to see him take an empty seat near the center of the table. He does a wave to everyone. "Hey. Sorry I'm late. I ran into one of those weirded out fairy paths. Took a bit, but we got through."

"Yes, but I'd rather not do that again. It did ruffle my fur." A female cat voice speaks in my head just before a grey Persian cat jumps up in his lap.

"Greetings, Keeper Troy and Cat Sorceress Miriam." He looks toward the grey cat. "Would you like a feline seat? We had to begin without you, I'm afraid." Geldon motions to one of the guards at the door.

"Carry on, please," answers the feline cat voice. "I'll just settle in Troy's lap. I don't want to hold up an important council." She nods to Brewford to her right. "Are we not always meeting during times of woe?"

"It seems that a sorcerer cat's time is never wasted on anything but unworldly messes. But it is good to see you again, Mir."

My eyebrows rise a bit by Brewford's tone. He actually sounded like he was being nice to her. Surprising.

"Well, yes, as we had mentioned before our Keeper from the European Realms entered, we will need to gather as many Crystal Keepers as possible." Geldon's voice quickly has heads turning back to him.

"May I suggest a possible plan?" It is Sydney. He leans in a bit toward the table.

"You are welcome to speak, friend Dragon." Geldon motions toward Sydney as he sits down.

Sydney nods to Geldon and continues. "I think an expedition is in order. An expedition to retrieve Crystal Keepers from the past and present needs to be organized. I know this might be dangerous with the paths in the state they are in. But repairs can be made along the way, and locations found that need further attention. I can talk to my fellow dragons on how to proceed. They can begin with repairs, but to retrieve the Keepers we need, an expert time guide will be needed."

"Are you suggesting." An elf speaks up. He looks like he is of a sand or desert region from his brown and red hair. His clothes are sand colored. He stands to continue. ". . . that time travel is necessary to find the number of Keepers we need?" He leans forward on the table as he looks at Geldon.

"Yes." Sydney's head swings toward the elf speaker. "I know it is risky, with the paths in their current state, but it may be the only way to find enough Keepers before Balkazaar gains enough power to be free."

"And who will lead this expedition into the past and present?" rang out a dwarf's voice.

"Who will be able to navigate the paths with the problems going on?" insists another elf.

"I will." Sydney answers with a simple knowing tone. "And I will need a Keeper that is familiar with the problem, and a Keeper that knows the time pathways who has traveled before." He looks first at me and then at the boy Keeper Troy. "And I think we should get started as soon as possible."

The Hawaiian woman stands. She has a strong, commanding voice as she begins. "I do believe the time gate in my realm will be helpful in gathering the Keepers. The volcanic action funnels enough energy to port several Keepers at a time. It should be able to accommodate a dragon guide with several Keepers."

"It is what will be needed Queen Pele." Sydney bows his head slightly. "I think it will be a good starting point for our journey. I do believe Wanda has her crystal pendant being repaired as we speak. Your Menehune should be able to put the final touches on it to make it capable of traveling through the Realms of Time. Keeper Troy can get his fitted there as well.

"Then it is decided." Geldon looks about the faces surrounding the table. "Keeper Wanda and Keeper Troy are appointed with the mission to travel in time to gather more Keepers to fight Balkazaar. If they travel to the Realm of Pele first, her people, the Menehune, can fit their crystals to help them travel to the past."

There are muffled agreements from the people all about me. I keep trying not to think about school or if I can travel in time, let alone that I am about to go out and save the world . . . again. Before I know it, I'm saying, "I know traveling in time, we could probably fix missing school. But I know I've been in the Fairy World for a while. Will someone be missing me now? Last time when I went to Ireland, it was not more than a few hours when it seemed like days here. How will the time travel thing work?" There. That might help distract how nervous I was feeling. Could I do it all?

If a dragon can smile, I think that is what Sydney is doing now. He begins with a chuckle. "It's simple. When you master time, there is a 'when' for anything. Too much jumping in time can cause a problem. But as long as you don't run into yourself too many times, there shouldn't be a time paradox. That is why most fairies only do short time travel. Dragons have always been able to navigate long time jumps. We live for so long, it is easy to keep track of the time pathways and where we are in different times. Mostly, we become familiar with several time passages. I'll lead us down several I know already. We should be able to pick up some Keepers until we have enough."

"But how do we know how many Keepers is enough?" I sort of blurt it out. I can't help it.

"When we start to feel a balance returning to the paths. Then, we should be able to gather and lock Balkazaar up for good." Castrotomas has a tone of authority in his voice. "But first you must gather them. The cat sorcerers can help coordinate and direct your energy."

"Then we'll blast Balkazaar back into his prison for good," interrupts Troy. "I'm in for some of that."

"Then, we will start to gather for this expedition." Sydney rumbles with satisfaction.

"I will be happy to equip our two Crystal Keepers with anything they may need," adds the Dwarf King.

"I'll lead them to my Realm of Hawaii," said Queen Pele. "There, we'll prepare them for their trip to the past."

I mind speak to Brewford. *This is going to get interesting real fast.* I turn to see Troy looking at me. I give him a nod and smile back. After all, when I really look closely, he is kind of cute. He looks back at me and winks. Yes, very interesting. I know I am blushing again.

CHAPTER 11

The Land of Queen Pele

I still don't have a real idea of how long I've been here in the Dwarf City of Galderon. But I'm going on a time adventure. I guess I am going to have plenty of time.

The Dwarf King is as good as his word. He equips Sydney with leather bags that will help carry food and materials. I've gotten my crystal pendant from the Dwarven master cutter. It looks so different in its new silver setting. It has a beautiful garnet set into the silver. The loop is etched with filigree decorations that line the silver work. I love it.

You okay, crystal friend? I ask the fairy within the crystal.

Yes, Wanda, she answers. *I've been transferred to a much safer crystal. It is sturdy and should lend me the power I need to aid you in your Crystal Keeper duties.*

Good. Because it looks like we're almost ready to go.

I have a new leather satchel complete with a loaf of dwarven bread, cheese, water skin, and a few apples from the surface. A dwarf comes running over to us, just as I look up from my pack.

"Where do you want your charts stored, Master Sydney?" She blurts out as dust stands in a cloud behind him.

"Please pack it in the satchel on my left side. Thank you, Phelix." Sydney does a bit of a shuffle to his left to give Phelix enough room to load all the charts without running into the side of the cave.

"Are you almost ready, Keeper?" Queen Pele is looking over all the things Sydney has to pack. "I know you want to confer with my people about your suspicions. It would disturb me greatly if you were rushed and didn't have what you needed."

"No." He looks over all the packs with a sniff. "I think this is the last chart. Where are Keeper Troy and Sorceress Miriam?"

Troy is making sure he has enough bread and cheese. Miriam's head voice rings with mirth as she slinks into the cave opening.

There is a shout from the corridor. "I have to make sure the food is all edible for our journey." Troy walks in with a great smile on his face. "I have to say, all the food I tested passed the test. I haven't dropped dead yet." He winks at me as he wipes his mouth with his sleeve. I smile back. I try to not get that flushed feeling when I look at him. After all, he is a Keeper like me. But he is definitely cuter than Justin Bieber. It is making it difficult to concentrate when I look at him.

I think we are all here, Master Sydney. Brewford's head voice is starting to sound like his old self, slightly annoyed, as usual.

"Then on the way to the paths, I guess," I say with a shrug and start to walk to the corridor.

"Wait, Wanda." Sydney's voice makes me stop in my tracks. "You should always let me lead in this adventure. The time pathways can be dangerous. Plus, we will be traveling to the land of Pele's people. She must guide us there first."

Well, I always hate waiting around. I nod and bow a bit as Queen Pele takes the position behind Sydney. After all, she is a queen. I guess that still tops Crystal Keeper in some circles.

We all fall into line behind Sydney. The queen is first, then me, followed by Brewford, Troy, and Miriam. We look like a little parade walking through the Dwarven castle. Servants and ladies stop to wave. We wave back. After all, that's what you do in a parade. We make it through the passages and back through the Hall of Flags. From there, we head into the streets down to the guild area, where we enter one of the buildings and approach an interior doorway. The double doors are gilded with gold around the edges, and glow slightly as I look at them.

Queen Pele turns to all of us before she speaks. "Here before us is the main passage out of the Realm of Dwarves. I will set the fairy paths to direct us to my home in the Realm of Hawaii. Be wary of the swirling motion as I reset the fairy path."

Queen Pele raises her hands and the doors open outward from the center. A light behind them starts to flash and strobe. Then as the doors open wider, it swirls into a light vortex. I'd seen one of these before. Balkazaar had made one and jumped through it, taking Eddie. That seemed like a long time ago. But it had only been about a week ago. I wasn't sure, except for the time I'd spent in the human world. The fairy world time is much harder to estimate.

The queen raises her hands again and lowers them back down. The swirling stops. A bright path lies before us, inlaid with bright clear crystals. Red garnets are wedged among the crystals, emitting a reddish glow. It is mysteriously beautiful and eerie at the same time.

I file in line through the doors behind the others. The ground is covered in a fine sand. It is like walking on the beach. I expect to see seashells next. After traveling for a while, shells start to appear in the walls and scattered on the sandy ground. A glow is in the distance, and I start to hear a roar. Well, more like a whoosh, sort of similar to waves hitting cliffs. I've gone to the beach enough to recognize the signs. But the fairy path lacked one thing, the actual water. Until we turn a corner.

We emerge from a cave onto a cliff overlooking the sea. The cave entrance is on an outcropping that has a narrow trail leading down a side ledge. Waves hit the cliffs below. A slight breeze moves the tops of the palm trees below us. It is so tropical and warm. The humidity feels like the steam while taking a shower. I've never been to Hawaii before. I don't think I am going to want to leave anytime soon.

"Aloha and welcome to the Big Island of Hawaii." Queen Pele turns to us, and we look off the bluff where we are standing. The water below looks deep blue. We can see a beach to our right that is a lighter blue. Turtles are on the beach. They seem content to lie on the sand. It all seems peaceful, as if nothing is wrong. I can totally forget why I am here.

But then I remember the mission for being here. I break the spell that is washing over me from the tropical climate. "Where do we go to get our crystals fitted, Queen Pele?"

"Come." Queen Pele motions us to follow. She starts down the path that leads down the side of the cliff. A slight breeze helps cool me down as we follow the steep trail to the beach. I try to avoid looking down the side of the cliff. I can hear the crash of the waves upon the rocks. It can tell me how high we are, without looking down. I focus on my feet and following the trail. We continue to head down toward the beach. After a few moments of focusing on my feet, I wonder where everyone is on the trail.

I look over my shoulder to see the Brew just behind me, followed by Troy and Miriam. Sydney is now bringing up the rear of our adventure party. I look back around to see the queen as she turns a corner that leads away from the beach toward the jungle. Bright flowers of red and white start to dot the path. Ferns and creeping vines cling to massive trees on all sides of us. The sun has trouble reaching us below the canopy of leaves. But the humidity is warm and comforting. It is like being rolled up in a warm blanket of mist.

A mosquito buzzes past my nose. Ick. I wave it away, only to have it quickly replaced by another. I was starting to feel hunted as we walked deeper into the jungle. Mosquitoes love me. I imagine red bumps all over my legs and arms. I swat one on my neck as I feel the familiar sting.

Wanda, are you all right? Brewford's tone of concern is touching.

"Not enjoying the welcome back to the real world, Brew." I swat another one on my hand. "Mosquitoes are attacking me. Do you have a spell or something to protect against mosquito assault?"

Alas, mosquitoes are a bit hard to dispel. It could interrupt the balance to drive them away with a blast or simple shield. We are soon off the fairy paths. They might be attracted to your energy.

Swat. "I guess that would explain a lot. They have always seemed to like me. I remember eating a lot of garlic bread at gymnastics day camp. Wish I had some now."

I take my hair out of its ponytail. It falls to its shoulder length around my neck. There. Hopefully that will help. I might swelter, but at least it might keep some of the mosquitoes at bay.

I look ahead to see Queen Pele turning onto another path. It is winding up a large mountain. Steam rises in the distance ahead. In fact, I can see a lot of steam ahead. The ground is starting to change, too. The jungle is starting to disappear and be replaced by black rock. Large stretches of it cover different parts of the land. It almost looks like tar, but then I see the frozen air bubbles in the rock. It looks like lava. We must be heading into the volcanic region of the island.

The trail starts to get dusty. The ground turns brown with scattered hunks of black rock lying in different areas. Soon, we pass some pools of water bubbling with activity. The smell of rotten eggs fills the air.

Yuck. I must have been having Real World return shock. Mosquitoes, egg-smelling pools of water. Double Yuck. I am thinking it might be better to head back to the beach. I clamp my nose closed with my fingers. At least that helps. I try to resist the need to ask "How much longer?"

Finally, the queen turns into an opening in a large cliff. It is hidden by a lot of vines and plants. They seem to part as she draws near. We follow closely behind. Sydney has to shuffle through. I hear a huff from behind me.

Do watch how you wave your tail, Dragon. Brewford dashes around me.

"Pardon me, Master Brewford. It is a tight squeeze. You have to give a dragon a bit of a break." He ends his comment with a chuckle. I hear a mental, humph from Brewford. At this point, I couldn't help myself.

I feel the resistance fail. "Are we all most there, Your Majesty?"

"We are almost there, Keeper Wanda." She doesn't stop as she answers. But I hear her as if in surround sound. Weird.

We have only gone another several feet when lights start to twinkle among the leaves and branches around us. They swarm like fireflies around the queen. Then, they break off in all directions. Some come over to me and land on my arm. Unlike the mosquitoes, they don't try to bite. In fact, the light dims, and I start to make out a tiny person with clear wings staring back at me.

"Welcome to the Volcanic Forest. The queen has asked me to show you where to get your crystal fitted for your journey." She seems smaller than the other fairies from my home realm. She is definitely brighter and slight of build. Plus, she is no bigger than a butterfly. She must be a cousin to the pigglewiggin fairies, and reminds me of them. There is a difference though. She doesn't need a bumblebee as her trusted steed.

"Hey, right back at ya fairy friend. Where to the nearest crystal repair shop?" I can hear Troy's voice booming behind me.

"Sounds like we both have found new fairy friends," I answer back. "Lead on, friend fairy. Let's get this party started."

CHAPTER 12

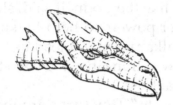

The Little Things

The fireflies start to swirl around me into a whirlwind overhead. Then, they head off down a path through the forest. I start after them with Troy right behind me. I could hear the swish of the branches as they smack into him.

"Hey, watch it. Haven't you ever gone hiking before?" He says as he stops a branch from hitting him in the face.

"Sorry. No, I haven't gone hiking before. Isn't there suppose to be a trail when you go hiking anyway? I've got to fight my way through first. But, I'll try to ease the branch back."

He comes up next to me. "Or we can try side by side. Might keep me from being blinded." We both reach for a branch at the same time, and there it was. A tingle.

"Sorry, I didn't mean to bump." I could feel myself turning red again. I hadn't talked this much to a boy before. Most of the time, I'm ignored. This was totally new territory. "I'm not used to working with anyone. Most of the time, I go solo. Well, until . . ."

I stop as the next branch swishes past me. Troy has to look back. "Until what . . ."

It is hard to think about it. But maybe we'll still find her if we can stop Balkazaar. "My friend, Eddie. She's another Keeper. She's the Crystal Keeper that Balkazaar took through a vortex."

He stops pushing back branches for a second, turns, and looks at me. "Well, like the Council said, she's probably being used for her Keeper powers to help Balkazaar escape. If we push on, finding Balkazaar might lead us to her." I smile.

"That's what I was thinking. We can stop him. That will definitely help her at least."

"If we're not too late." Troy turns around and starts up the trail, this time pushing the branches back so I'll have a chance to get by. "See this is how it's done."

"Yeah, I think I've got it now."

"When we get back, maybe we can go hiking together. It would be nice to hang out with another Crystal Keeper." He stops to wait for my answer.

"Yeah, I'd like that," I answer quietly. There. That was easy. Troy doesn't seem like the other boys I know. He is actually being nice to me.

The firefly-like fairies swoop up into some tree branches and circle around the trunk. They hover and stop in the center. Then they fade into the trunk. I knew that trick. I study the tree carefully. It has a lot of branches that look like they've grown into each other, forming the main trunk. I've never seen a tree like it before. But I shrug my shoulders and take a deep breath. I walk into the trunk.

And I hit my nose. Ouch. I start to rub it, but it starts to throb as Troy says behind me, "Why did you do that?"

Still rubbing my nose, I answer, "It worked back home. It's how I enter the fairy realm there."

"This is another fairy realm, Wanda. Plus, that is a Baobab tree. You're from another realm, and it probably doesn't recognize you. You have to ask permission first."

I scrunch my face to help minimize the pain a bit. "I wish someone had told me."

Troy folds his arms. "So how long have you been a Keeper?"

"Since June."

"That's just four months." He shakes his head. "Come on, I'll show you how to enter a foreign realm."

He walks up to the trunk and knocks three times.

A high-pitched voice asks, "Who goes there?"

"Keeper Troy and Keeper Wanda wish to enter your realm. May we enter?"

"Permission granted."

"All you have to do is ask permission?"

"Didn't you know? Asking nicely can get you into most places."

The trunk starts to waver in the middle, and a swirl starts to form. Troy steps through. This time, I test with my arm. I stick it through slowly. I feel a pull on the other side. I stumble through falling right into Troy. He catches me just before I face plant into the floor. "Thanks," I stammer at him as he helps me stand up.

"Good morrow, Keepers."

I look over to the voice and see a small person rising up from a little workbench. Small shelves line the inside of the trunk. All sorts of silver findings and crystals cover the shelves. Candles hang lit in holders on the walls. I feel a bit like a giant with all the small tools lying about. He continues to work on an object at his table. The tap, tap, tap of his small hammer echos off the walls of the wooden hideaway.

"The tree sprites have let me know you need some further work done on your crystals."

He pauses a moment to look up from his table. "May I see them?"

"And you are?" I ask. Really, I was in a good mood now that we were getting somewhere.

"Fieldsbark. I'm a Menehune Master Crafter. Handcrafted jewelry items that need magical adaptations are a Menehune specialty. Sometimes, the dwarves send their specialized work to us. I'm guessing you need it all done very soon. They usually send me rush jobs."

I nod as I lift the necklace from about my neck and hand it to him. He has a large nose, with wrinkles that give him a distinguished, weathered look. He takes the pendant and picks up an eyepiece from the table. It looks like a jeweler's eyeglass. After placing it up to his eye, he holds the pendant closer to him.

"Fine work. The dwarves are experts at fashioning a Crystal Keeper pendant. I think this looks like Master Cutter Larson's work."

"I think that was his name. I broke my old crystal and needed a new one. I had to save the crystal fairy within."

"Hmmm." He nods and turns it over in his hands. "Not bad for a rush job." He holds the crystal and closes his eyes. He takes a deep breath and the crystal starts to glow brightly. It lights his face slightly with a bluish glow and dims.

"Your crystal fairy seems pretty pleased with the new crystal. I'll just add a few things to help you navigate a Time Gate. Ah." He sets the crystal down and starts looking over the shelves. "There's one right there. I think an amethyst set next to the garnet should do the trick. Should keep the balance of energy while traveling through Time Gates." He takes a small purple stone and sets it next to my pendant. "Now for yours, young man."

Troy slips his pendant over his head and hands it to Fieldsbark. He turns it over and over. Then, he holds it up close, looking through the jeweler's loop. "Hmm. This is special work. What fairy realm are you from, lad?"

"England, sir. Near Avebury."

"I thought it looked English. Might even be a bit of Druid design to it."

"Yes. I have a Druid teacher."

"I thought so. Right. I think the best thing to add to yours would be a citrine stone. Yes, a nice, yellow quartz should help you navigate the Time Gates."

Fieldsbark reaches onto another shelf and picks up a small yellow stone. "Now, if you both come back in a few hours, I'll have these ready for you."

"What do we do in the meantime?" I ask.

"Let's go do that hike, then?" Troy claps his hands looking at me expectantly.

"Sure," I answer. But I was thinking, "I thought you'd never ask."

Next thing I know, Troy is dashing up a trail and I'm trying to keep up. I'm wading in mud that is up near the top of my shoe. Who knew Hawaii could be so wet? Brewford and Miriam decide not to come. Mud and cats don't mix. I don't blame him. Relaxing in the trunk hideaway seems better than hiking through this muck. Maybe hiking and me don't mix.

"This is brilliant." Thwack. Thwack. Troy is doing the trail blazing. I think I flunked hiking in Brownies. Troy had naturally taken over the lead for the hike. Thwack. Thwack. "I've never seen trees like this before."

I take a look around. The trees are magnificent. There are huge trunks at their centers. Some are as tall as redwoods or sequoias. Vine-like bundles twine together to form them. I think they are unique to Hawaii. The flowers are amazing, too. There are all kinds. I think I like the big red ones the best. It is like walking through a big tropical botanical garden. Every once in a while there is a trickle of water or a spring.

Then we hear a roar up ahead.

"That's got to be a waterfall." Troy takes off down the trail. I try to keep up, but his steps are two steps to my one step. His stride is huge. I just don't walk that fast. I end up getting a bit behind on the trail. That is our mistake. There is a flash off to the side.

Suddenly, a pasty bald man is standing right in front of me. He has red eyes and black clothes. Wispy fog or smoke wafts around him. He holds out his staff to the side, as if he owns the forest. His thin, black mustache twirls up as he smiles at me. He is completely blocking my path. "I've been expecting you to try something, Wanda. Little did I know you'd bring another Keeper with you. I couldn't have asked for more. Thank you."

"Balkazaar," hisses between my teeth as I stop dead in my tracks. Now what?

CHAPTER 13

Guilt and Sorrow

"You always have great timing, Balkazaar." Really. I was mad. I didn't even think to be scared. I was sick of this guy ruining my day, my life, and for taking my friend. "So, what have you been up to? Sick of Eddie yet? Can you bring her back like a good villain, or do I have to get rough?"

He gave a chuckle at that. "Really, Wanda. Of all the Keepers, I seem to like you best. I think it's because you seem to watch so much of that contraption in your world. What is it called, a television? I think it gives you too many ideas. Really, you should study more of the books Castrotomas and Brewford give you." He twists his mustache. "I'm not your average villain, you see. I have plans for you."

I fold my arms. "Oh, really. What might those be? Swooping me through a vortex too? I think I'm on to your tricks. Plus, if you keep showing up like this, I'll be able to dodge anything you've got. You don't seem to be able to come up with good plans."

There. Hopefully, some of the TV dialogue I hear on the countless shows I watch is coming in handy. After all, I doubt he's seen the same shows. And I need time to figure out what to do. Why is he here? Where is Eddie? And can I get him to tell me more? No, he can't be that stupid. But I know he is up to something. Doesn't the villain in a lot of cop shows tell what he's going to do before he does it? Like he's gloating or something?

"Really, Wanda. You should know me better than that. After all, luck has been on your side." He raises an eyebrow. "Until now."

"Hey, Wanda, are you coming or not?" shouts Troy behind Balkazaar. It is like stop motion. Balkazaar turns to swing at Troy with his staff. The staff lights up with sparks. All at once, they zap at Troy. But Troy has definitely been a Crystal Keeper longer. He raises his hands at the same time Balkazaar raises his staff. A shimmer goes up around Troy, and sparks bounce off of him. "Run, Wanda. Run back to camp."

I don't have to be told twice. I glance back for a sec to see sparks flying around the both of them. It is only a moment's hesitation. A scene pops in my head of Obi-Wan Kenobi battling Darth Vader. Didn't he shout the same thing at Luke? I know it is old-school logic, but I don't know how to deflect bolts from a staff. Troy seems to. So I ran.

Maybe if I can get to Queen Pele, she can help. Or Brewford and Sydney. But the one thing about mud and me—we don't mix. I slip and fall right on my butt. Mud doesn't help with an escape.

I can still hear zing, zing, and a crash behind me. I pick myself up and try to keep going. I have a spectacular amount of mud all over me now. I try to go to the side of the trail with the least mud. All of a sudden I hear, "Keep going. He's right behind me." It is Troy. I can hear the pounding of his feet. The mud is behind us, and he has almost caught up with me. At least he didn't see me fall, hopefully.

I keep going, arms pumping. The trail soon changes from jungle to beach. We start to leave the forest area just as I feel I can't run any longer. I slow down and say, "Troy, I think we've lost him." I stop and bend over feeling exhausted from the sprint. I don't hear an answer.

I look behind me. There is no one there.

That's two Crystal Keepers missing. Brewford's head voice is full of concern and worry. This is new for even him.

"Unfortunately, Balkazaar is getting quite a collection." Sydney answers with a puff of smoke from his nostrils. I haven't seen any fire yet, but I figure it might be brewing somewhere inside him.

I would say it wasn't the best idea to go hiking without your crystal pendants. It left you vulnerable to Balkazaar, Brewford says with a bit of a huff. *I wish you'd let me know they weren't with you when you left.*

"I'm sorry, Brew. I thought we'd be fine. We just went for a hike." I am trying to remain calm. "I didn't think it was a problem." I start to have tears well up. "I didn't mean for anything to happen." And that let the floodgates open. I start a good old-fashioned cry.

I think it is just too much. First Eddie, and now Troy. Every time I make a friend, they disappear. I am beginning to think maybe I should just stay a loner. It seems to be better for other people.

"Now, now, Wanda," There is a comforting grumble to Sydney's voice. "You couldn't have known that your crystals were prime guardian tools. You've only been a Keeper for a few months. This is a large crisis for you to be pulled into. Troy should have known better, too." This is followed by a little snort. "But then, I'll tell him that when I see him again."

I sniff. "Maybe Balkazaar didn't take him. Maybe he's somewhere along the trail or . . ." I sniff again. "Or he just might have gotten lost, and he'll be back in a second."

Queen Pele interrupts, "I have my people out and about looking for him. They have found nothing but footprints around where the battle took place. There are also some down the path you both took. Then there is nothing. It's as if he disappeared from that spot."

I wipe my nose with the back of my hand. Not glamorous, I know. But I've reached my breaking point. I've been feeling so confident until this point.

There is something we can do. Brewford's head voice resounds with new hope. *The mission will carry on. Queen Pele, continue your search, but the pattern most likely is that Balkazaar has taken Troy to continue with his plans of escape. There's only one way to stop him.* He stops for a moment. Brew looks to see that he has all of our attention. *We head to the past to try to gather the Keepers we need, and stop Balkazaar. He must not gather enough Keepers before we do. It will be a race . . .*

". . . against time. Yeah, that is funny, Brew." I give a quick snort laugh. "That's a good one." Sometimes ill-timed humor makes me feel better.

I didn't mean it to be funny. Brew sounded indignant with my answer. Oh well, I don't think he understands human humor, or at least my humor, sometimes.

"The Master Cat Sorcerer is correct," responded the queen. "We will carry on the search, and you will gather the Keepers. It is the only way to stop Balkazaar."

"In time." I smiled again. The blank stares tell me I was wasting my humor again. "Okay, I think a plan is the best way to approach this, too." In fact, I am starting to feel better. A plan gives me the feeling we are doing something. "Sydney, you'll still guide me to the past. Brewford, could you come, too? Believe it or not, you actually do give good advice."

The Brew sits up a little straighter. His tail twitches from side to side. "Of course. At this time of crisis, it would be wrong to let you down, Wanda."

"Then it's settled," Sydney answers. "We carry on with the main plan. But we must keep in mind Balkazaar knows we are up to something. We must be more alert and careful as we proceed."

"Agreed." Brewford nods. "I think the first thing is to retrieve your pendant and meet at the Time Gate. Queen Pele, could you help Wanda with that? I think our last Keeper will need to be constantly escorted until we enter the Time Gate."

"Of course, Master Brewford. I am happy to help. I will alert you if anything else is found letting us know the location of Keeper Troy." She nods to Brewford and motions toward me. "Come, Keeper. Let us see if your pendant is ready for your journey through the Gate."

I follow the queen down the path toward the Baobab tree grove. It seems like days ago, not just hours. Maybe it was days. Time while traveling in the fairy worlds could be different. It didn't always feel the same. Would I ever see Mom again? I was even starting to miss my little brother, a little. I know he messed up when he broke my crystal, but I always forget to put my stuff higher when he is around. And the whole fairy thing made me forget where we were in his rotation schedule with Mom and Dad.

I walk along the trail looking at the strange vine-covered trees. Yup. I am going to have to be more thoughtful when it comes to Balkazaar and working as a Keeper. I'm not going to let Balkazaar catch me off guard again.

The trail is less muddy going back to the workshop. We enter behind the queen. The Menehune looks up from his bench. He is still holding a small hammer over a crystal and chain. "Oh, yes. You are back. The crystals are fitted for the Time Gate. Oh, but where is the other Keeper?" He looks around behind us. "Is he not picking up his as well? I need him to try it on to see if it is properly tuned to him."

I can't say anything. A lump forms in my throat as Queen Pele speaks. "Keeper Troy has had a run-in with the Dark Sorcerer Balkazaar. He seems to have disappeared, and we are having everyone search for signs of him now."

Fieldsbark lowers his head. "That is news of bad hearing." He looks over at me. "He seems a competent Keeper. I hope he is able to escape from the evil Balkazaar." He shakes his head. "But come, Keeper, I do have yours ready."

I walk forward and reach for my pendant. It has a newly set garnet in its silver fastening. It winks red light at me. "It's beautiful." I pull it back over my head. I feel connected with my crystal fairy instantly. Waves of comfort flood my mind.

The tingle of the crystal fairy's head voice rings in my head. *It is not your fault. We will find Troy and Eddie. Sometimes the way to solve a problem is to head toward anything that might lead to an answer.*

I smile at her thought. "Yes, answers aren't easy."

"A bit of wisdom can take a lifetime to learn, Keeper. Feel comforted you've learned some today." The queen places her hand on my shoulder. "Let us get you prepared for your journey. After a meal and some rest, you will feel ready."

"Now that I think of it, I could use some food. I can't remember how long it's been since I've eaten."

"Fairies don't replenish ourselves the way humans do. We will forget your basic needs if not reminded." The queen motioned for me to follow her.

Now that I think about it, I could use the bathroom, too. After all, you have to take care of yourself before you can save the world.

CHAPTER 14

Back to the Past

Food can make you feel so much better. I feel like I can conquer the world. Well, at least I felt I could stop Balkazaar.

But I feel as if I am standing on the edge of a cliff with someone behind me giving quick pushes to my back. I am easing into unknown territory. What will it be like to travel in time? When are we going? How will Sydney navigate the Time Gate? What will we find when we get there?

We are at the place where Sydney will charge and open the Time Gate. His dragon bulk has just fit in a glade about as big as a small house. Newly grown grass covers the meadow with wildflowers sprinkled throughout. It is a blanket of green and white. Surrounding us are Baobab trees. A chorus of birds chirps in the background.

We are standing in a circle waiting for Sydney to begin. I look around me. Next to Sydney is Queen Pele with the Master Crafter Fieldsbark to her right. Brewford stands next to him, and I close off the circle. Sydney starts to puff smoke into the center. His nostrils flare as he breathes a stream of fire into the center. I don't feel much heat from the flame, but smoke swirls upward. He repeats the process three times before a funnel appears in the center. A steady light is in the small tornado.

"The vortex is open in the center of our circle." Sydney's voice sounds strong and sure. I wish I could speak like that. "Just give it a bit of time to spin and grow in size."

We watch it grow until it is finally the height of Sydney. At that point, there is a loud crack and the smoke bursts open to reveal a large globe of light filled with swirling flashes of green and blue. "It is open. The Time Gate is ready." Sydney's voice is very pleased. "I will enter first, followed by Wanda. Brewford shall bring up the anchor position." He turns to the queen. "Once we have all gone through, you should be able to close the Gate safely, Queen Pele."

The queen nods. I could barely hear Sydney over the whooshing and whirling sounds the vortex is making. Every once in a while, a static-like crackle comes from the sphere.

"Are you sure it's safe to go in?" I say eyeing it thoughtfully. "It seems like a giant typhoon in a ball."

"I assure you it is quite safe and stable. Let us proceed." Sydney moves toward the spinning sphere. As he approaches, it spins less and widens. The opening glows brightly as he starts to walk in. Yet, he pauses with just his tail sticking out for a while. Then, his tail pulls into the oval after him.

"Humans first," directs Brewford.

Okay, so this is why Crystal Keepers shouldn't hesitate. I start toward the spinning sphere, and watch the sparks fly outward. I remember smashing my nose on a tree trunk not to long ago. I rub my nose for momentary sympathy. "You sure it's okay?" I look back at the Brew.

"Yes, Wanda. Time Vortexes are usually a little more erratic than regular travel vortexes. It's okay. I will follow right behind you."

Just as Brewford speaks, there is another loud crackle. We all turn to see what has made the noise. Again, did I mention hesitation could be a Keeper's worst enemy?

Balkazaar stands not but a few feet across from me. He aims his staff at the vortex.

"Jump now, Wanda, or it may be too late." Brewford's head-voice scream is muffled by the noise of the vortex as I jump in. Again, I am in for some slow-motion magic. As I enter the vortex, I can still see on the other side. Balkazaar is hitting it with a bolt. Then, he aims his staff at the Brew. That's when everything goes crazy inside. I start to spin and turn. Sparks turn and spin around me, forming another tornado within the globe, except this time I am in the middle of it. I can see nothing outside, and I feel like I'm falling.

Everything goes black except for the spinning bolts around me. The spinning sensation surrounds me. I get dizzy and have the sensation of throwing up. Except I can't get grounded enough to do anything but a few dry heaves as I try to regain my balance. And that was the problem. I am spinning and falling down at the same time. I imagine this must be what it feels like to jump out of a plane, except I am moving nowhere. Well, I'm not moving anywhere I can see and feel.

Then, I feel the thump. My eyes are closed as the spinning stops. When I open them, I can't believe where I am. I've fallen into the middle of my quad area at school. And I am the only one here. I don't see anyone about, except it seems to be daytime. The sun is out and a cool breeze blows across my face. I can feel the freshly mowed grass where my hands braced myself from the fall. At least I assume I landed. I had one knee up and the other in a partial sitting position.

Just then, I hear the click, click of shoes coming down one of the corridors. In fact, it sounds like high heels banging away. I look over, following the sound, and see it's a lady wearing rimmed glasses. She is dressed in one of those retro dress suits from the 1980s. I've seen a few of them in reruns of *Dallas* and *Saved By the Bell*. She has on a powder-blue silk blouse to match the grey color of the suit. She spots me and heads my direction.

"Young lady, what are you doing? You should be in class by now. The bell rang at least ten minutes ago." She looks at her watch. "Did you check in the office for a tardy slip?"

"No, not yet." I get up and brush off some of the grass. Time for some quick thinking. "I must have lost track of time studying for my test next period. I'll go now."

"Yes. I'm sure your homeroom teacher will want to know you're here by now. Off you go." She motions me toward the front office. That's when I get a good look at her face. It is Mrs. Wilkinson, my social studies teacher. But she is much younger. There are hardly any wrinkles on her face.

No. That can't be possible, unless she's had serious plastic surgery in the last few days. Of course, then it dawns on me. Maybe that wasn't a retro suit design she was wearing. Maybe this is the 1980s. "Thanks, ah, Mrs. Wilkinson. I'll get to the office now."

I head off the quad grass into one of the side passages that leads to the front office. I want to figure out where or rather, when I've landed, before she asks me too many questions. I keep a look out for Sydney and Brewford. I'm not sure if they've made it through the vortex. I keep picturing Balkazaar aiming his staff at the Brew. I am starting to worry something has really gone wrong.

I make it to the front office and go straight to the secretary's desk. It isn't Mrs. Blane, our regular secretary. This secretary is a different lady with brown hair and dark brown eyes. Her hair is in a feathered style that flips far too much and seems to be plastered in place with hair spray. I can smell the residue from where I'm standing in front of her.

She looks up from the file she is working on. "Can I help you, dear?" Her voice is that adult super sweet, but annoyed I've interrupted her.

I figure she's one of those grown ups that treats you like you're still six or something. I think that's one problem that bugs me in Junior High. Being treated like you are still in elementary school. I give a scrunch to my face as I think of what to ask. Then I spot it. Right behind her desk is a calendar with happy-looking children reading a book. The month is a clear beacon to where I landed. It says: October 1983.

"Um." I am in a moment of speechlessness.

"Speak up, dear. I don't have all day. Were you late to school? Do you need a tardy slip and pass?"

I nod my head completely dumbfounded. I feel frozen to the spot. 1983. What am I going to do? I have no idea where Sydney is or if Brewford has made it through. As far as I know, I am alone, in 1983.

The only thing I can think of is to nod.

"Okay, dear. I'll write you a pass. Katrina? Could you come here a moment?"

From the back room, a girl comes out from working at what looks like a really old copy machine. Well, it looks old to me. It seems to take up all the room in the backspace of the office. The secretary turns around to talk to the girl. "Katrina dear, could you take, um, what was your name did you say?"

"Wanda."

"Yes, Wanda to her homeroom class." She hands me a pink slip of paper. "Here is your pass."

I accept it, not knowing how to continue. As I'm thinking of an answer for the secretary, I get a good look at Katrina's face. No. It can't be. But I realize she'd gone to school here too, thirty years ago. I try to remain calm as one thought comes to me.

Mom?

~

Acknowledgements

I'd like to thank all of my friends and family for all of the support they've given me while writing the Crystal Keeper series. I started writing back in 2005, and there has been such a road of accomplishments. You helped shine light at the end of the tunnel for me to succeed.

Thank you to my parents for helping me when I struggled as a young child with hearing problems. I always had difficulty with writing, and my mom and dad both supported my explorations with stories, poetry, and essays. Thank you, Mom and Dad. It's a hard job being a parent.

Next, I'd like to thank my Inner Circle of friends that give constant feedback as my books go through the lengthy process of writing. Thank you, Lisa. You are the Queen Latifah to my Emma Thompson inner writing self. Just continue to remind me to "Just Keep Swimming."

To many of my Renaissance Fair friends, thank you for your support and interest, and the lasting friendships that are a second family.

To Rich Wallace, thank you for the awesome, brilliant cover art that keeps bringing my characters to life in each book. You give a new dimension to the series.

To my editor Shelley Holloway, thank you for all of the hard work and constant emails to make this book beyond awesome. Your comments helped guide me through the jungle of crazy verb tenses and narrations.

And last of all, thank you to all of my readers for entering the world of the Crystal Keeper. Thank you for making it possible for me to keep writing.

For more information on my writing, my blog, and other Crystal Keeper Chronicle books, please visit my website at: http://www.tiffany-turner.com

Enjoyed the book? Want to talk to other readers about the Crystal Keeper Chronicles? How about writing a review at: http://www.amazon.com or http://www.goodreads.com

Plus, join Wanda in the fourth book of the Crystal Keeper Series, *The Lost Secret of Time*. Will Wanda be trapped in the 1980s? Can her mother help her find a way to stop Balkazaar? Find out the answers in the final book of the Crystal Keeper Chronicles.

Would you like to have your very own handmade crystal pendant, just like a Keeper?*

Cut out and send in the coupon below, along with $2.95 for shipping, to:

Tiffany Turner
Crystal Keeper Pendant
6081 Meridian Ave. Ste.70
Box 116
San Jose, CA 95120

You will receive an official Keeper Certificate signed by the author Tiffany Turner and fairy Queen Lillith.

FREE HANDMADE CRYSTAL-KEEPER PENDANT

Name: _____

Address: _____

_____

_____

*This offer is for first-time Crystal Keepers only.

Remember to include $2.95 for shipping and handling.

Would you like information on other Crystal Keeper Chronicle Books?

Yes or No (*Please circle one*)

If you have already signed up as an official Crystal Keeper, Queen Lillith is guarding your membership. Wear your crystal proudly.